PUFFIN BOOKS

Becoming Julia

Chris Westwood was born and brought up in a West
Yorkshire mining village. He spent three years as a journalist
with the *Record Mirror* before studying film and TV
production for two years at Bournemouth Film School. His
first book, *A Light in the Black*, was published in 1989 and he
now writes full time.

Other books by Chris Westwood

BROTHER OF MINE
CALLING ALL MONSTERS
A LIGHT IN THE BLACK
PERSONAL EFFECTS

Chris Westwood

BECOMING JULIA

PUFFIN BOOKS

PUFFIN BOOKS

Published by the Penguin Group
Penguin Books Ltd, 27 Wrights Lane, London W8 5TZ, England
Penguin Books USA Inc., 375 Hudson Street, New York, New York 10014, USA
Penguin Books Australia Ltd, Ringwood, Victoria, Australia
Penguin Books Canada Ltd, 10 Alcorn Avenue, Toronto, Ontario, Canada M4V 3B2
Penguin Books (NZ) Ltd, 182–190 Wairau Road, Auckland 10, New Zealand

Penguin Books Ltd, Registered Offices: Harmondsworth, Middlesex, England

First published by Viking 1995
Published in Puffin Books 1996
1 3 5 7 9 10 8 6 4 2

Filmset in Ehrhardt

Made and printed in England by Clays Ltd, St Ives plc

To
Sandra Ann Longfield,
with love and best wishes

1

Maggie had been trawling the small ads for days before she saw the one she'd been looking for.

Wanted, it said. *Girl, young prof or student, pref non-smoker, for own room in 3 BDR flat in Riverside area. £160 pcm. Gas C/H included. Phone/electricity extra. Call Linda on 694–9073 after 6pm.*

Circling the ad with a red ballpoint pen, Maggie put down the newspaper and checked her watch. She still had an hour to kill, though she'd better not wait until six before calling, by which time the line would be jammed. She'd tried two other numbers yesterday, only to find the flats had been claimed within minutes of the *Evening Post* hitting the streets.

She made coffee and searched Ceefax for news. There was still no update on the local talking point of the moment: the disappearance of a college student, Julia Broderick, who had last been seen outside a night-club in Leeds late the previous Thursday. Of course, people always suspected the worst, but the news item Maggie had read didn't say whether Julia had been entering or leaving the venue at the time, or just passing by. Perhaps she had left town on a whim without telling anyone.

By five-thirty, Maggie was growing restless. Her

parents would be home soon and she didn't want to make the call while they eavesdropped at the doorway and silently pleaded with her not to leave home. They already knew she planned to, but it would still be easier, she thought, to reassure them that what she was doing was right once she'd done it. The telephone sat on the low glass table beside the TV. She lifted the receiver, newspaper in hand, and dialled.

Typically, the line was engaged. It was yesterday all over again. Someone, somewhere was this very minute snatching the room from under her nose: how dare they call before six! That was so underhanded! She hung up, cursing her luck, just as the front door slammed and her mother came breezing into the hall. Through the living-room doorway Maggie watched her shaking water from her umbrella, stamping her feet on the doormat.

'I'm home, Mags,' she hollered up the stairs.

'In here,' Maggie answered. 'Looks like you got caught in a downpour, Mum.'

'Did I ever.' Her mother stood in the doorway, patting her rain-beaded hair. 'Just look at my perm. Sometimes I wonder why I bother. So, tell me: how was your first day in employment?'

'Exhausting. Anyone who says library work is a quiet, cushy number for people who love books ought to try a little hands-on experience. I've spent just one afternoon organizing the shelves in the junior section and it's going to take me a week to clear the muck from under my nails.'

'Well, that's life in the real world for you. Blood, sweat, tears and dirty books. What are the people like?'

2

'Very helpful. Very sweet. I think I'm going to enjoy being there.'

'That's great!' Her mother was such an enthusiast. 'Was I interrupting you just now, Mags? Are you expecting a call from some boyfriend?'

Maggie was still crouched over the phone. 'Not exactly. You're forgetting I split up with Ian two weeks ago, but I'm just about to make a call. Would you mind making coffee? My last one has turned cold.'

'The instant I'm out of these wet things. I'll be down in a minute.'

Waiting until her mother's footfalls had faded up-stairs, Maggie pushed the living-room door to, then returned to the phone and re-dialled. This time there was a ringing tone, and after three or four pulses a girl's voice answered, reciting the number in a mild Australian accent.

'Is Linda there?' Maggie said.

'Yes, she is. Speaking.'

'I'm inquiring about the room in your ad.'

'Ah. Who isn't?'

'Don't tell me it's gone. I'm too late again, aren't I? I called just a minute ago and your line was busy.'

'No kidding. It's been ringing continuously for the last hour, believe me. But the room hasn't gone yet. There's a lot of interest, but the last couple of calls were from fogies who didn't want to share with people like us.'

Maggie was intrigued. 'People like you? What do you mean?'

'Well, I have to come clean. This is Bohemia here. We both like our rock music loud and we're not really looking for anyone too straight-laced, if you follow.'

'I think so. But the ad didn't mention anything like that.'

'Of course not. Can you imagine what the landlord would say? If you're still interested —'

'I am, I am.'

The girl called Linda paused for a moment. 'Tell me a little about yourself first.'

'There isn't too much to tell. My name's Maggie Waverly. That's Madelaine, not Margaret, but Maggie rather than Maddie, if you follow. I've just finished school and started work, and I'm looking for a place nearer the city centre. I speak two languages, hate soap operas on TV and I like *my* rock music set to stun.'

'So far so good. Can you cook?'

'A little.'

'Well, we could use someone around here who can. When *I* get started, most of it ends up on the walls or the floor.'

'Any chance I could see the place?' Maggie asked.

'Sure, but . . .' Linda fell silent for a moment. 'There are two people coming to view in the morning, quite early. Between you and me, they both sounded like duds on the phone. The thing is, Maggie, we're only allowed to *show* the flat. Everything else is in the hands of the accommodation agency. And if either of these people tomorrow morning likes what they see . . . Do you think you could come over tonight? I mean, I know it's dismal out there, but we might just sneak you in by the back door.'

'I'll be there whenever you're ready.' Maggie could scarcely believe her luck.

Linda said, 'Make it an hour. That'll give me time

to scrape the lasagne off the linoleum. I'll give you the address if you have a pen handy.'

She dictated while Maggie scribbled the details across the newspaper's property column. By the time she'd hung up, Maggie was buzzing – but her mother was standing in the doorway, a steaming cup of coffee in each hand.

'I couldn't help overhearing,' she said. 'Just the last part, that is. Are you serious about this, Mags?'

'Pretty serious, yes. But I have to view the room yet. You can't tell everything just from an ad in the paper and a voice on the phone.'

'Of course not. You have to see for yourself. Does it sound like a decent place?'

'It's a share in Riverside, quite a trendy area now. And the girl I just spoke to, Linda, sounds terrific.'

But her mother looked crestfallen; she always did whenever conversation switched to Maggie's fleeing the nest for a place of her own. She had wept, Maggie remembered, the day her elder brother, Jonathan, left home for London. Now, as she handed Maggie her coffee and reclined on the sofa, she said, 'Is it wise of you to go out in this rain, though? You're liable to catch your death out there tonight.'

'It's a chance I'm willing to take.'

'Oh, well, that's entirely your choice.' Her mother's lips were forcing a smile her eyes were unable to match. 'If you're sure this is what you want –'

'It is.'

'We've been over it several times already, I know. But I do worry it might be too great a financial burden too soon for you. This is only your first day at work, remember. Just think what you might do if you saved a while longer.'

'I *have* thought. I'd still be at home and I'd be missing out on too many other experiences. Besides which, the rent's pretty reasonable.'

'In quite a hurry to leave us, Mags, aren't you?'

'Mum, can we talk about this later?' Maggie was on her feet and tugging on her coat in the hall in an instant. The last thing she wanted was to hurt her mother's feelings, but in truth she *was* in a hurry to leave, if only to escape conversations like this. It was the same old pressure: don't take that step, stay here, you don't know what's out there in the big bad world. You'll catch your death out there, so you will.

'I'll be back before nine,' Maggie said, and took up the dripping umbrella on her way out the door.

Outside, the wind was rising and the rain seemed to be settling in for the night. The streets, even at this hour, were already dark and deserted. Overhead, the loaded sky pressed down above the roof-tops as if a great unseen hand were forcing it. Thrusting the umbrella forward into the wind, Maggie hurried along Calderwood Grove, a street of grey pebble-dashed houses. Television images bloomed in cosy living-room windows, a different talking head inside each one she passed. In this, a fist-waving American senator; in that, a tight-lipped newsreader unable to cheer up his audience. As she rounded the corner on to Fitzroy Street for the bus, she thought she heard footsteps following her and, straining against the wind and the umbrella, twisted around to look.

There was no one in sight. What she'd heard was probably water overflowing a roof-top gutter, or the echo of her own steps trapped in the rain. Was she nervous? If not, then why was she imagining things? She knew these streets like the back of her hand, and they were safe, always had been.

'Don't be a fool,' she said aloud, the sound of her own voice reviving her, spurring her on. If her nerves were fluttering, it was only because she'd wound herself up about the flat, which – especially after speaking to Linda – seemed an opportunity not to be missed. She shouldn't allow her parents to make her feel guilty. Even if they meant well, they should at least try to understand how badly she wanted this.

On Fitzroy Street, the traffic crawled past towards the city centre, windscreen wipers at full tilt. Rain swirled in the headlights, dashed the glass walls of the bus shelter as Maggie ducked inside it. She was shaking off her umbrella when a pale shape along the street to her right caught her eye as it fluttered along the gutter towards her.

At first she thought it was a page of an old newspaper. She caught a glimpse of a headline in large bold type and an image beneath it, an artist's impression of a face. Then, as the paper unfurled itself at her feet, she saw that the headline said:

MISSING.

It was a poster, not a newspaper, and there were more words below the portrait. None of them registered with her, because the face, a girl's, nearly took Maggie's breath away.

Initially, she was sure it was her own. It couldn't be, but even if this was an artist's impression, not a photograph, the likeness was striking. She was stooping to pick up the sopping poster when a gust of wind snatched it out of her reach. Shivering, she watched it flash along Fitzroy Street, under the wheels of a car, where it was torn to shreds. *You're liable to catch your death*, she thought, and then jumped at the sudden crash and hiss of noise to her immediate right. The bus doors sighed open, and Maggie stumbled inside, cold, dripping wet, grateful to be in the light among people again.

2

The girl who opened the door looked as if she'd just seen a ghost. If this was Linda, she was almost exactly as Maggie had pictured her, though perhaps even more colourful. Her hair was blonde, wild and back-brushed and she wore an oversized chunky white sweater with black leggings and Doc Marten boots. The instant she laid eyes on Maggie her mouth sagged open.

'My God,' she said.

'Hi, we spoke on the phone before. You must be –'

'Linda. That's right.' She stood there uncertainly, not offering to open the door further.

'Is everything all right?'

'No. I mean yes, of course. I'm sorry.' She slapped her forehead with the heel of a hand and at last stepped aside. 'What am I playing at? Get yourself in here. It's only that when I saw you I thought . . .'

'Yes?'

'Well, you're saturated, just look at you! I shouldn't have dragged you all the way here on a night like tonight.'

'I'm determined, if nothing else,' Maggie said.

'Let's see how determined you are once you've seen how we animals live. I haven't cleaned up or anything.'

'Except for the lasagne on the floor, I hope.'

'Ah, yes.' Linda smiled. 'Except for that. Follow me.'

As they mounted the first set of stairs, turned a landing, mounted another set, Maggie said, 'You're Australian, aren't you?'

'How did you guess? Yes, from Perth. I hope you don't hold *Neighbours* against us, is all I can say.'

'No, I'm no bigot. I believe we're all born the same in the eyes of God.'

They both laughed, crossed the next landing, took the next flight of stairs.

Linda said, 'The skies there are so blue and so high they steal your breath. And the landscape . . . You must be wondering what on earth I'm doing here, wrapped up like a mummy to keep out the English climate.'

'It did cross my mind.'

'What's good enough for Germaine Greer's good enough for me, ha ha. The truth is, I'm studying to become an actress. This in my first year at drama school; couldn't get into RADA or any such thing, but I still wanted to study in England instead of at home. Why the hell not? A long time ago I decided that whatever I do, I *do* want to travel, I don't want to miss anything the world has to offer. If I can learn to act *and* circle the globe in the bargain, believe me, I'm going for it. By the way, pleased to meet you.'

Stopping at a door on the upper landing, Linda turned to shake hands, and it occurred to Maggie how small her own world seemed by comparison. Linda had travelled half-way across the world without a pang of doubt; and here was she, just a bus ride from home and guilty as sin for snubbing her folks! Suddenly she knew she was in good company; this scenario had a feeling of rightness about it.

'This is our humble abode,' Linda said, gesturing theatrically as they entered a spacious living-room area. There were huge potted plants in corners, posters of Madonna and Val Kilmer on the walls, and apart from a pair of muddy shoes in the hearth and a discarded bra on the back of one armchair, few signs of the wreckage Maggie had half-expected. 'This is where we watch TV, drink wine into the night and pour out our hearts and souls to each other,' Linda went on. 'Over there is the phone. I guess you know how to use one. And in here –' She swept open a door to the left and snapped on a light. '– is the kitchen. Frozen pizzas, mildewed hummous and green milk in the fridge. Everything works.'

'It's fine,' Maggie said. She could scarcely contain her excitement. 'Which is my room?'

'*Your* room? I like your attitude. You've practically moved in already. This way.'

A wardrobe, an oval-mirrored dresser and a three-quarter-size bed with a night-table beside it were the only items in the bedroom Linda took her to next. The carpet looked new and warm, red curtains hung in the windows, the white walls were clean except for a scattering of tack marks where posters had been. It had possibilities.

'Next,' Linda said, leading the way. 'The only problem with the bathroom is that the lock needs fixing. That's fine as long as the pad is girls only. It could be a problem if your boyfriend comes round and forgets to knock first.'

'I don't have a boyfriend. We – we split up a couple of weeks ago.'

'That's a shame. Or maybe not. Are you better off without him?'

'At first I thought so. He was seeing someone else, so I gave him his marching orders.'

'Good for you. No less than he deserves. No second thoughts now. Never rewind the clock.'

Linda thrust open the bathroom door.

'Do you mind?' A raven-haired, pale-skinned girl perched on the edge of the bath, wearing only a towel. She was painting her toe-nails crimson. 'What happened to privacy here?'

'Privacy? No such thing. This is Christine,' Linda said. 'Christine, meet Maggie. I'm showing her the penthouse.'

'Oh, hi,' Christine said, glancing up from her work. Her features seemed to stiffen for a moment, her black eyes flickered. Was it Maggie's imagination or did a look pass between her and Linda? 'I hope Linda hasn't put you off,' she said. 'She's such a slob, it's going to be tough to lure anyone else in here, but take it from me, she isn't as bad as she seems.'

'I'll talk to you later,' Linda said, wagging a finger.

Maggie said, 'As a matter of fact, I'm more than happy with what I've seen. Is the landlord OK?'

'The landlord's a mystery,' Christine replied. 'Actually we deal directly with the agency, and the landlord never comes into it. Some guy called Newsome, as far as I know. Hey – would you like a towel? You're dripping on the carpet.' She plucked a spare from the edge of the bath and tossed it. 'Here. Catch.'

Maggie plucked it from the air, thanked her, began

mopping her hair. As she did so, she became gradually aware of Christine watching her in silence; in fact, she was staring. Her dark eyes were puzzled.

'What's up?' Maggie asked. 'Linda gave me that look when she opened the door a few minutes ago. I've got the strangest feeling you two know something I don't.'

'It's nothing,' Linda said. 'It probably wouldn't mean anything to you anyway. It's just that we had someone else in here before –'

'The girl whose room you're interested in,' Christine said. 'She cleared her stuff out only last week. But when I saw you just now – I could've sworn she'd come back.'

'She looked like me? That's curious.'

'Not exactly like you,' Linda said quickly. 'But there are similarities. You definitely have her colouring.'

Maggie finished drying her hair, folded the towel carefully over a heated metal rail on the wall. She had seen something herself tonight which had made her react the way these girls had just now – the face on the poster. 'Who was she?'

'A local girl,' Linda said. 'Perhaps you even knew her; a very popular girl. This time last week, she told us out of the blue she was going away to marry; moved out the next day just like that, no planning, no warning. Then, Thursday night, she dropped in to see us – she wanted to make sure there were no hard feelings, I guess. As if. She was on her way out for the evening and didn't stay long. That was the last time we saw her. Her parents have been trying to reach her, but we don't know where she is.'

'Maybe you read about her in the newspaper,'

13

Christine said, recapping her bottle of varnish. 'There's been so much speculation. In fact, the police were here asking questions earlier, not that we could tell them anything we haven't told you. Her name's Julia Broderick. She's been reported missing.'

3

Maggie had just enough time before work to visit the accommodation agency in a cramped, dark suite above a hairdresser's on Kirkgate. She filled out the landlord's contract, wrote a cheque for the deposit and the first month's rent. After that, all she required was references. Joyce Durham and Kate Bradshaw at the library typed them out for her during lunch. She was moving.

And moving in by the weekend. She came, her father driving her, with books and CDs in boxes, clothes bunched into plastic shopping bags, large arty prints in clip-frames for the walls of her room. Her father, to Maggie's relief, had been quietly supportive of the move from the start, or at least less emotional about it than her mother. She'd expected opposition from him, but it hadn't been forthcoming. 'My honest opinion? It's high time you started making decisions about your own life,' he'd told her as they drove to the flat.

She was delighted, too, to see him take Linda and Christine in his stride, joining them in a relay up and down the stairs with her things, small-talking over coffee before leaving to collect his wife from her sister's in Roundhay. In the end he seemed almost reluctant to go. When Maggie walked him to the car he was beaming and nodding approvingly. The girls had won him over, thank goodness.

'We'll see you again soon?' he asked hopefully, peering at her over the thick rims of his glasses.

Maggie spread out her hands like a modest fisherman. 'Dad, I'm only this far from home. What do *you* think?'

'Your flatmates are very – colourful,' he said, selecting his words with care. 'I approve. They seem lively and intelligent girls. They'll be good for you. You'll be happy here.'

'I know. And I hope you'll tell that to Mum.'

'She won't need convincing. On the face of it she may seem sad to see you go, but she's secretly delighted, take it from me. If this is what you want, it's what *we* want. As long as you're sure you can afford it.'

'Thanks. And to think I expected –'

'Yes? What *did* you expect?'

'Nothing. I'm glad things worked out this way, that's all. It's a great old house, don't you agree? I'm sure it has a wonderful history. Good and old and bristling with character. Home from home.'

'Home from home. Right. I like that.'

They kissed and she watched him into the car, waved as he sped along the street, then turned back up the drive to the house. As she did so, a swift small movement at a first-floor window caught her eye; a curtain flapping perhaps, or someone passing the window in the instant she looked up.

Upstairs, the girls were already unpacking her bags. They were down on their haunches in the living-room, stacking books into piles, loading CDs on to shelves.

'Like a couple of eager domestics,' Maggie said. 'What a great help you two are.'

'We're just nosy,' said Christine. 'I *love* going through other people's things, and yours are no exception. Do you have any diaries?'

'If you have, keep them padlocked,' Linda said. 'Hey, I heard this book was the *end*! Can I borrow it?' She held up a spine-cracked *Something Wicked This Way Comes*. 'It'll make a change from my usual reading.'

'*Just Seventeen* and *My Guy*,' Christine confided.

For a moment Linda looked tempted to throw the book at her. Then she thought better of it. 'I was thinking more of Nietzsche and the complete works of Shakespeare. I'll have you know I'm an artist and intellectual giant.'

The telephone rang. Maggie jumped.

'Ah,' Linda said. 'The outside world! So there's life beyond these four walls after all. Maggie, why don't you get it while we see what else you've brought us? If it's Marcus, my *beau*, tell him no, he can't come over unless he brings flowers and chocolates.'

'You're mad,' Maggie said. Laughing, she raised the receiver. 'Hello?'

The line was silent, but it wasn't dead, she was certain that someone was there. Perhaps whoever was calling could hear her but for some reason couldn't make themselves heard; faults of that nature sometimes occurred on the phone at her parents'. 'Hello?' she repeated, then heard the click as the connection was severed.

'Who was that?' Christine wanted to know.

'No one. That is, I think someone was listening but not talking.'

'Freaks,' Linda said. She was musing over a book of quotations, not lifting her eyes from the page. 'The world is full of weird-minded people. We had a spate of those calls a month or so ago, didn't we?'

'I think what it is,' Christine said, 'is that sometimes would-be burglars phone at random just to check if anyone's home. I know it upset Julia when it happened before. She got it into her head that those calls were meant for her.'

Linda said, 'Whether or not they were, she needn't have worried. This flat is pretty secure. The doors and locks are solid, the walls thick. Ha!' She had just turned a page of the book of quotations. 'See if you can guess who said this: "Don't knock masturbation; it's sex with someone I love."'

The others burst out laughing.

'See where the intellectual giant's real interests lie?' Christine shrugged. 'Come on, Maggie, let's kick your room into shape.'

Finished unpacking, they spent the afternoon at the city centre's indoor market, housed in a huge, ornate stone building, once a Victorian warehouse. They bought Pepsis in a café that, to Maggie, felt steeped in market life: the smells of cigarette smoke and greasy food, oversized men with shirtsleeves rolled up to expose tattooed forearms, women wearing gaudy make-up and strong perfume, runny-nosed children, the cheapest prices in town.

Here and elsewhere, as they drifted from stall to stall, she began to feel vaguely prim and stiff beside the others: Linda with her heavy boots, leggings and motorbike jacket; Christine all in black, her eyes mascara'd, her fingernails painted. Her own tastes had always been conservative, after her mother's, but now was her chance for change, even if she couldn't yet see herself in ankle-high Docs. At a trinket stall she bought tiny pineapple ear-rings and a red bandanna for her hair, while Christine slipped a silver death's head ring on her own wedding finger. At a T-shirt stall she deliberated between plain yellow and plain white, finally settling on black with the slogan: *I used to be conceited but now I'm perfect*. Linda purchased a gift of dried flowers in a basket for Maggie's room, Maggie found muslin for the windows and, on a junk stall, a framed black-and-white still of Marlon Brando in *The Wild One*. Tired and close to broke, they started back as the market traders began pulling down the corrugated iron shutters on their stalls. They pooled the last of their money for wine, cheese and baguettes along the way.

When they reached the house, a young man was idling on the doorstep. Tall and unshaven, with his long brown hair tied back in a pony-tail and intense dark eyes that would've have made Maggie instinctively turn and run if she'd been alone, he appeared to have been waiting for some time.

'Where've you been?' he said to Linda, a tremor of annoyance in his voice. 'I've been calling you all afternoon.'

'Whoops,' Christine said quietly to Maggie. 'Boyfriend trouble.'

'Don't tell me. I know all about it. Boys are jealous gods. You shall serve no one else but me.'

'Where does it look like we've been?' Linda said, offloading bags into his arms before tinkling her key-ring towards the lock. 'Picking up men, of course. Painting the town red. More to the point, where are our chocolates, you oaf?'

'Who're you?' he said to Maggie, so directly she faltered before stepping nearer. Christine squeezed past him, following Linda indoors.

'I moved in today,' Maggie said. 'Julia Broderick's old room. You must be Marcus.'

He nodded, and forced a smile. Oddly, she thought, he didn't seem surprised by her resemblance to Julia – if there was a resemblance – as the others had. 'Ah. I'm sorry about just now. I've been freezing to death here for nearly an hour. Pleased to meet you. You must be Maggie. Linda told me about you.'

He put out his hand, and Maggie shook it. When he didn't let go, but kept a firm grip on her fingers as he pressed his lips to them, she didn't know how to respond. Did he greet every friend of Linda's this way? Then again, any boyfriend of hers was most likely an actor too: kissy devils, the lot of them, Maggie imagined.

'Pleased to meet you too,' she said, pulling away. Suddenly flustered, she blundered past him, through the front door, in an effort to catch up with the others. As she followed Christine and Linda into the flat, she felt an inexplicable flush of relief. First appearances could often be deceptive – certainly that had proved to be true in Ian's case – so she would reserve judgement on Marcus for now. After all, she'd only just met him. There was no reason on earth why he should have made her feel so uncomfortable so soon.

4

On the outskirts of the city, at the point where the river curved beyond the black sprawl of factories to the open country, a blond-haired boy sat on the bank by a tree, his parka closed to the throat, his fishing-rod idle at his side. It didn't matter how many times he'd been told there was nothing to catch here or, at least, that any fish he hooked from the brown foamy water was most probably toxic, he wasn't impressed: there was life in this river, he was certain. Fair enough, his only catch today had been a half-rotten tennis shoe, probably a child's, the laces long gone. But there were riches in these dark depths, no question, and this was his patch and he was sticking it out. The promise of rain from the gathering of clouds above the grey hills beyond the city only strengthened his resolve.

Down below him, below the steep muddy bank, the red float bobbed and surfaced again. The boy turned another page of the Arthur C. Clarke paperback he'd packed with his lunch-box for the day. Some distance beyond the river the soccer stadium's floodlights reached for the sky. Nearer, a local train crawled wearily past on its way towards Sheffield. In the water, the float dipped again, this time violently. It didn't resurface.

At first he failed to notice it. In his mind he was somewhere else altogether; somewhere out there, travelling at warp speed, doing battle beyond the stars, colonizing far-distant planets. It was the noise of the sudden wild unfurling of the reel that made him sit up with a start. Beside him, the line was feeding out at an incredible rate.

He dropped the book and seized the rod, his heart pounding. It was impossible to tell, until he began to reel in, whether what he'd hooked was a sprat or a shark; he couldn't gauge its weight until then. Lifting the rod from its rest, he flopped down on his backside, digging his heels into the mud for purchase, and began to backwind. As he did, the end of rod dipped sharply, forming an archer's bow. Come on, he thought, not daring to say it out loud; come on in, let me see you. What a moment it would be when he slapped the slimy beast on the kitchen table tonight: imagine his folks, imagine his brothers, their eyebrows raised, their mouths agape. The ultimate Told You So!

He'd now reached the point where the line jarred and tightened, where he could begin to sense the size of the creature he was dealing with. It was heavy, for sure, but as he strained to reel the catch home, he couldn't help feeling that something was wrong; this was not the way it should be. The river looked choppy, but mainly because of the rising wind, not because the catch was struggling. In fact, it didn't seem to be resisting at all.

Briefly, the line caught on a broken branch down at the water's edge. The boy let the line slacken, jerked it free with a sharp flick of the rod and, shifting his position on the bank, began to edge downwards, feeling his way through the mud with his heels.

There was still no resistance from whatever it was he'd hooked. Surely, if it had been a fish, it would have broken loose while the fishing gut was snagged. There was something else down there, something large and dark which had lodged against the bank near the base of the tree. He tugged at the line and the shape shifted. This, then, was the thing he had caught.

His heart was in his throat now. Already he felt faint with anticipation. He wanted to see and yet couldn't bear to go on looking. Even when the shape in the water, tossed by the current, began to roll over, he didn't know whether to scramble down for a closer inspection or up the bank and away to safety. On impulse he gave the line one last, firm tug.

It was then that what he was seeing made total, terrible sense. The dark shape in the river rolled over fully and everything, every detail, immediately fell into place: the black sleeveless dress which the girl was wearing, her lifeless white limbs twitching in the water, the marks on her forehead, worst of all, her still-open eyes.

Dropping everything, the boy set off up the bank, driven by panic. He was screaming for help as he went, screaming though he was too far away from the city to make himself heard, screaming because the river seemed determined to suck him back into it. He was raking back mud by the handful, his wellington boots skidding out from under him. Before he reached the top of the slope, he slid and collapsed flat on his stomach, the strength knocked out of him by shock. It was all he could do to push himself forward again and keep moving, running towards the city, not looking back.

Three hours later, Detective Inspector Penhaligon stood on the very spot where the boy had slipped and grimaced at the splashes of mud on the bottoms of his M&S suit trousers and his ruined black brogues. The fishing tackle lay where the boy had dropped it; the pages of the Arthur C. Clarke novel flapped in the wind. Nothing had been touched except the body. They had taken her away two hours ago. Now, Penhaligon flinched as the camera crew prepared themselves for a take, the interviewer thrusting a microphone towards his face.

'Ready, sir?' the reporter asked. 'Can I just get a level?'

Penhaligon cleared his throat, straightened his back. He was keen to create the correct impression: outraged, but in complete control. 'Testing one two, one two,' he said.

The journalist nudged the microphone nearer. 'OK, that's great, here we go. Inspector, can you describe, first of all, what happened here and when?'

'Well, the story we have is that around midday today, somewhere between twelve and twelve-thirty, a local youth was fishing this stretch of the river behind me . . . his tackle is still here as you can see . . . and he hooked some article of clothing that the girl was wearing. He immediately ran to the nearest telephone for help. Quite a fair distance from here.'

'Are you able to confirm yet whether the victim could be the missing girl, Julia Broderick?'

'Jesus,' Christine exclaimed. 'It is. It is. I just know it.'

'Quiet,' said Linda. 'Wait and hear what he says.'

D.I. Penhaligon went on, 'At this time, before a formal identification's been made, I'm not in a position to confirm or deny that. All I can add is that, our feeling is, this girl had been in the water for several days and in the first instance she does fit the physical description we have of Julia Broderick.'

'Oh Jesus,' Linda gasped, gnawing both her knuckled fists at once. She glanced anxiously at Christine, then at Maggie, her eyes glistening. Marcus, on the couch beside her, slipped a comforting hand round her shoulders.

'Is the cause of death known at this time?' the reporter said.

'First impressions would lead us to assume that she drowned. Whether or not that was the result of an accident isn't yet clear. We still have to establish where she entered the river. And there are certain details – I'm afraid I can't be more specific than that now – which would tend to suggest foul play.'

'What's with this pussyfooting?' Christine demanded of the TV screen. 'You wouldn't even be *there* if this wasn't foul play!' She looked at Linda, whose hands were still at her mouth. 'Good God, she *was* murdered. Can't you feel it?'

Linda nodded. Maggie, cross-legged on the carpet in front of the TV, hugged herself to stifle a cold shiver.

'Do you have a message for the public?' the journalist asked. 'Is there anything they can do?'

'Lock your friggin' doors,' Christine said.

'Well, we have reason to believe the body is that of Julia Broderick, but until a formal indentification has been made, we can't confirm this. However, members of Julia Broderick's family have already been contacted. But as far as the general public is concerned –' D.I. Penhaligon turned his head slightly, staring directly into the camera. 'If you knew Julia Broderick, no matter how vaguely, and whether or not you had any contact with her recently, please come forward. Even if you were interviewed by the police several days ago, we'd like to hear from you again. Anything you know, regardless of how trivial it seems, could be of vital importance.' He turned back to face the reporter. 'We'd also like to hear from anyone who saw a girl fitting Julia's description during the last few days: her photograph has already been circulated. We're working on the assumption that she was last seen at night. She was wearing a black party dress, the sort of dress she might have worn to a disco or night-club, perhaps. There are two points I'd like to make about this, if I can . . .'

The reporter nodded, twitched the mike.

'First of all, she wasn't dressed for the season. That is, this is a particularly severe October, very wet, very cold, but the dress she had on was lightweight, really a summer evening dress. As yet, we haven't located a coat or sweater or any other article she might've worn over it. We'd like to hear from anyone who has found such a garment. However . . .' Penhaligon cleared his throat before continuing. 'If she didn't have a coat – and we have to assume she needed one at this time of the year – then it may be that she was travelling by car. If anyone gave a lift to this girl, or saw her getting into or out of a car, it's most important that you contact the police.

'Finally, there's another question mark concerning her footwear. The girl was wearing black, canvas boat shoes, the slip-on kind. Again, I'd associate shoes of that kind with summer or at least indoor wear. But the problem is, would she really wear cheap boat shoes with a stylish, and probably expensive, dress to a night-club? For all we know, this could have been her kind of fashion statement, but there may be people out there who –'

Without warning, the screen flickered and turned hazy with snow. The sound collapsed to white noise.

'Damn this TV,' Linda said, on her feet, impatiently thumping the top of the set with a fist.

'Check the aerial,' Marcus said. 'This usually happens when the aerial falls out.'

As the news team packed away their camera and sound equipment, the reporter said, 'Inspector, just one thing off the record. About the marks on the girl's forehead ... There's a rumour circulating that they were made by a pencil or crayon.'

'Until we've heard from the labs, it's impossible to say which,' Penhaligon said. 'My assumption is that they were caused by lipstick or something similar; at least something water-resistant.'

'Can you say whether or not some kind of message had actually been *written* on the girl's forehead? Two words, to be exact ... And, if so, what those words could've been?'

'I'm sorry, I really can't confirm anything of that kind at this stage, on or off the record. Better to wait and see what develops. Now, if you'll excuse me . . .'

Without another word, Penhaligon fought his way up the bank, wiped his mud-caked shoes on the grass, and headed back to the car that awaited him.

5

The report switched back to the studio, where the presenter began a recap on the Julia Broderick story. It was a story that had travelled way beyond local speculation and gossip now; watching it unfold, Maggie felt she'd stumbled unwittingly into a TV whodunit. When a photograph of the missing girl flashed on the screen, she sensed the others stealing glances her way. Or at least Christine and Linda were: Marcus's attention was fixed defiantly on the screen.

The news came to an end, the weather report started. No one moved for minutes. At last, rising wearily as though her body had doubled its weight, Linda turned off the TV. 'I think I'd better open the wine now,' she said, fumbling her way to the kitchen.

Christine stared after her as if trying to decipher a cryptic message written on the kitchen door. Then she stood up, tight-lipped, her eyes brimming with tears, swallowing hard. 'Excuse me,' she said, and ran to her room.

The sound of the door slamming shut sent a wave of cold air through Maggie. She looked at Marcus, who was gazing in the general direction of the blank TV screen, not seeing her.

'This is dreadful,' she said weakly. It sounded pathetic, such a dumb understatement.

'Poor kid,' he replied. Even worse.

'Did you know her well?' she asked.

'Fairly well. I thought she was very bright and very beautiful. Everyone who knew her thought that. She didn't have any enemies. She wasn't the kind that made them.' He spoke, she thought, in a trance-like state, his eyes far away, his voice slow and dreamy.

Shivering, she dragged the cuffs of her cardigan over her fists to warm them. 'I think,' she began, not knowing what would come next, still awkward in Marcus's presence. 'I think I'd better check on Christine. I'll be back in a minute.'

Marcus didn't so much as acknowledge Maggie or glance her way as she got up and rounded the sofa where he was sitting, overstepping his outstretched legs. Was he purposely avoiding looking at her? Perhaps she was reading too much into his behaviour, or lack of it. After all, this was a terrible moment. Perhaps Marcus, much like herself, had been rendered light-headed and mute by the news.

She tapped lightly at Christine's door, then pushed it slightly ajar. Christine lay perfectly still, face-down on the bed, chin resting on her forearms. She sniffed and glanced up as Maggie entered, pressing the door silently shut behind her. Christine's face was streaked with mascara tears.

'Can I join you?' Maggie asked.

'Sure. Come in.' Christine rolled on to her side as Maggie pressed her weight on the edge of the bed. 'I'm OK. Just a little upset.'

'You must've been very close to Julia.'

30

'We both were. She lived here for almost a year. That was what was so surprising about the way she upped and left. My God, what a first day this must've been for you. I'm so sorry.'

'Don't apologize,' Maggie said, proffering a handkerchief from her cardigan pocket. 'Here. It's clean, you can use it.' She waited while Christine finished dabbing her eyes, then she said, 'Can we be sure the girl on the news was really Julia?'

Christine nodded. She didn't seem to need to consider it. 'Can I tell you something, Maggie? This will sound very off the wall, but I'm missing a pair of black pumps.'

Maggie looked at her incredulously.

'You heard me,' Christine said. 'I mean, not that they were stolen or anything. Julia needed to borrow them one night for an aerobics class she took every Thursday. She said, I think, that she'd left her Reeboks at her boyfriend's down in Cambridge. She used to travel there every other weekend to see him. Sometimes he came up and stayed here. When she left, it was such a spontaneous, rushed thing that I suppose she never thought to return them.'

'And the dress? Did Julia own a dress like the one they described?'

'I'm sure I'd remember if I'd seen her in that, but I don't. She spent all her money on clothes, though. She coveted Katherine Hamnett and Givenchy, never had her nose out of *Vogue* and *Cosmopolitan*. She couldn't afford that stuff, of course, but she did have taste, she liked to be noticed.' Christine turned the mascara-smeared handkerchief over in her hands, thought briefly about handing it back, then folded and set it down on the bed. 'Tell me, Maggie, why would anyone want to hurt her? She never made anyone hate her in her life, I swear. She wasn't the kind to make enemies.'

'That's exactly what Marcus just said.'

'What does he know?' Christine fell silent. After a moment she gently took Maggie's hands in her own. 'Listen, I know this probably won't make any sense to you yet, but . . . stay away from him, Maggie.'

'From Marcus?'

She nodded, purse-lipped. Her eyes were ablaze. 'What I mean is, don't get too friendly, keep your distance.'

'That's easy,' Maggie said. She was a trifle bewildered. 'To be honest, he does make me edgy. He seems cold.'

'Oh, that's just his manner. He can be very affectionate when you get to know him. That's half the problem, in fact.'

'Christine, what are you saying?'

But before she could answer, there was a knock at the door, and it swung open, and Linda stood there, her face the colour of chalk. 'Is everything OK with you two?'

'Yes. We're just fine.' Christine managed a smile. 'We were airing our sorrows, that's all.'

'Come out here and drown them, then. I have the wine open.'

'I'll be there right away. Maggie, you go ahead.' Christine gestured towards the door.

Casting one furtive glance back at Christine, Maggie rose from the bed and, with some reluctance, followed Linda from the room.

6

'I'm sorry, Mrs Gardineer, but these books are long overdue. You're going to have to pay a fine.'

Mrs Gardineer glared at Maggie as though Maggie had just insulted her honour. 'Fine? Why should I have to pay a fine? These books weren't even mine in the first place. They were my husband's, God rest his soul. They were gathering dust in the house, wasting space. If you did but know it, I'm doing you a favour, clearing them out.'

'I appreciate that, really I do.' Maggie was doing her best to seem cheerful, though she'd already been warned about Mrs Gardineer. 'They must have been lying about for a fair old time, though. Three years is just a little longer than –'

'There's no need to be facetious, my girl.' Mrs Gardineer, silver-haired and grey-eyed, utterly insane, lifted her black umbrella from the counter and trained it on Maggie. 'I didn't come here out of the kindness of my heart to be insulted by the likes of you.'

'No one's insulting you, Mrs Gardineer. Excuse me one second while I find out what's owing.' Skimming the electric-light pen over the bar-codes on *The Old Man and the Sea* and *Cannery Row*, checking the tally on the screen, Maggie licked her dry lips. 'Would you prefer to pay by instalments?' she said.

'This is hopeless.' The mad woman rapped the counter with her umbrella. 'Let me speak to the manager.'

'The manager's at a meeting this afternoon. Perhaps Mrs Durham can help?'

Mrs Gardineer clucked her tongue, gave a long, emphatic sigh, rolled her eyes to the ceiling for Maggie's benefit. For one brief moment, Maggie wondered how it would feel to leap clear of the counter, fasten her hands on the mad woman's throat, squeezing until she turned blue. 'Mrs Durham?' she half-whispered, half-called across the library. 'Can you spare us a moment?'

It was Maggie's first day at the service point, and until Mrs Gardineer's appearance it had been plain sailing. People, generally, had been kind and forgiving of her faltering mistakes. Now, those few customers not already staring her way stopped their browsing to do so as Joyce strode over from the Languages section.

'Ah, Mrs Gardineer, how good to see you,' Joyce gushed, and tipped a sly wink in Maggie's direction. 'What's the problem?'

'This young upstart has no respect for the dead,' Mrs Gardineer asserted. 'My poor husband borrowed these books just weeks before he passed away.' She pursed her lips and crossed herself. 'And now that he's gone and I'm returning them, of my own free will, she expects me to bankrupt myself by paying some outrageous fine. She tramples over his memory for the sake of a few days' oversight.'

'Three years,' Maggie said quietly.

'There she goes again,' Mrs Gardineer said. 'Did you hear that? No respect for anyone. Argumentative too.'

'It's all right,' Joyce said to Maggie. 'I'll deal with this.'

She took Mrs Gardineer to one side for a moment. They spoke in hushed voices, the old woman shrugging, waving her pale, long-fingered hands, sneaking the occasional dark look in Maggie's direction. At last, without another word, she returned to the counter, snatched up her umbrella, and marched from the library.

'I told her that this time it'll be all right,' Joyce said. 'Hell, I'd rather pay the fine myself than listen to the old hag for another minute. Let the Council count its losses.' She gave Maggie a quick, broad smile and went back to work. Maggie breathed a sigh of relief as the browsers returned to browsing and the silence resumed.

Most of them returned to browsing, at any rate. At the far side of the library, however, where the Psychology and Social Studies sections were, a young man stood watching her. He looked, at first glance, like a train-spotter, with spiky, unevenly cropped hair and small round glasses of the kind John Lennon had worn. He had on a khaki army jacket and blue jeans and tattered sneakers, and didn't turn back to the shelf until it seemed to occur to him that Maggie was returning his stare.

She had seen him in here before, one day last week. She remembered because at the time she'd been at the service point, watching and learning as Kate Bradshaw checked out customers' books. The train-spotter's books had struck her as being anything but light reading: *Fear and How to Cope With It* and *The Other Side of the Mind*, among others. There were some minds it would be better not to see the other side of, she thought.

Maggie returned to the computer, exited the screen of unreturned books, looked up to find the young man already at the service point, three hefty hardbacks stacked in front of him.

'Hello,' she said. 'How are you?'

'Fine, thanks.' The train-spotter smiled, fumbled, hunched his shoulders. The books he had selected were *True Crimes: Profiles of Six Mass Murderers*, *Somebody's Husband Somebody's Son* and *Ed Gein: Origins of a Serial Killer*. As he pushed his library membership card towards her, she noticed his name, Patrick Carver. She was tempted, as she ran the light pen across it, to comment on how appropriate that was, given his tastes in reading, but after Mrs Gardineer's earlier performance it was probably better to say nothing.

Instead she said, 'I've seen you in here before, haven't I?'

'That's right. You're new, aren't you?' He didn't seem able to make eye contact with her. He just stared fixedly at his books as she checked them out. 'I hope the old woman didn't upset you. She does that to everyone sooner or later. She's . . . she's almost legendary here.'

'I think I can cope with her, thanks. As long as she doesn't come in too often.' She passed Patrick Carver his books.

'Well,' he said, his lips twitching into a smile. He still wasn't looking directly at her. 'I'll be going then.'

'See you again soon. Looks like you have your work cut out for you in the mean time.'

'Beg your pardon?'

'All this reading, I mean. You're going to be very busy.'

'Oh, that. Oh, yes.' He was blushing. 'This is part of a personal project for college. I'm studying psychology there, you see. In case you were wondering.'

'I wasn't,' she lied. 'Don't forget your card now.'

'Oh, right. Thanks.' Sweeping it up from the counter, he nodded goodbye and hurried on his way, head down, clutching the books to his chest. What a curious little character, Maggie thought, watching him go. It wouldn't have taken much – the sudden raising of her voice, a pointed question or two about why he *really* wanted to read those books – to make him leap out of his skin. What did it take to create such a nervous, insecure young man? Perhaps she should read *The Other Side of the Mind* too.

Between three-thirty and four the library filled with school kids, the youngest accompanied by parents. Some of the eldest Maggie recognized from her final summer, the summer just gone, as fifth and lower-sixth formers. A couple went to work on the microfiche; others rifled the CD collection or occupied tables to conspire over homework; the majority took charge of the Junior section.

A line formed at the service point, and for half an hour Maggie was working flat out, the constant bleep of the computer lulling her to the edge of hypnosis. As the rush died down, she glanced across at the large main doors to see Christine trooping in, a spring to her step. She looked healthier than she had at the weekend, her complexion clearer, her eyes brighter. If the shock hadn't passed yet, at least she was in control again. When, on Sunday, it was announced that Julia Broderick had been positively identified by her family, both she and Linda had reacted to the news in the same accepting way. They had known it was coming.

'I was just passing,' she said, unhitching her shoulder bag, flopping it down on the counter. 'My fashion class finished early and I wanted to see how the other half lives. Personally, I always fancied library work. All that peace and quiet, the smell of old books, an environment where I could put my feet up.'

'If only,' Maggie laughed. 'I'll have you know I dream about the same desert island all day.'

'Actually, there was something I wanted to say.' Christine rested her elbows on the counter and leaned nearer. 'It's something and nothing, but I didn't want to let it pass. There were things I told you on Saturday night that were – well, I needed to make clearer.'

'Such as?'

'You know. Things I said about Marcus. Hints I dropped. And since you never brought it up again –'

'I didn't think it was my business to.'

'The fact is, I was blowing off steam emotionally. I was hitting out for the sake of it.'

'That's OK. I understand.'

'No, you don't, you don't really, which is why I had to tell you this. I should've explained myself better in the first place. Marcus is basically OK; I mean that. But there are times when I swear Linda would be better off without him. You probably haven't noticed, but he gives her an awful rough ride. He's very tough on her, very selfish.'

Maggie regarded her blankly for a moment, then had to break off as a mother arrived with a stack of six picture books for her daughter. When she'd gone, Maggie said, 'Marcus is a two-timer, is that what you're saying?'

'Marcus has a roving eye, let's put it that way. Once in a blue moon it gets the better of him, but he always comes back to Linda in the end.'

'And when it does get the better of him, is Linda aware?'

'She suspects. Once, as far as I know, he came clean and apologized, and they split up for a week and a half and then sort of fell together again. Not that I know *everything* that goes on between them.'

Maggie was livid. 'Why on earth does she put up with him? When I told her how Ian had treated me she spoke as if behaviour like that was unacceptable, as if she'd never tolerate it herself for a minute.'

'She wouldn't if she thought he was serious about what he was doing. She's pretty broad-minded at the best of times, Linda is. But at least you understand now what I meant by keeping your distance from him.'

'I think so.' Maggie considered for a moment. 'But you haven't explained why this flared up on Saturday, why the news report made you angry at Marcus.'

'I thought you'd have worked that out for yourself,' Christine said. 'The only time Marcus became serious – I mean properly serious – about anyone else besides Linda was when Linda went back to Australia in the summer. When he got himself involved with Julia.'

'You're joking.' Maggie looked at Christine open-mouthed. She was not joking. 'Marcus and Julia?'

'We ought to be doing this over a beer or two,

hadn't we?' Christine said. 'This is hardly the time or the place for a bombshell, is it?'

'All men are bastards,' Maggie said quietly.

'Amen,' Christine said. 'But it takes two to tango.'

'Does Linda know?'

'She must do, but it isn't something we've ever discussed. I've tried to protect her the best way I could. On the surface, she's always so confident, so outgoing, but underneath she's basically fragile, and since she was close to both Julia *and* Marcus, you can imagine how she would've taken the news. Perhaps now, now that Julia's gone, we'll talk it through. God knows, I wished I could've told her at the time, but more than anything else I wanted not to see her hurt.'

'But surely she suspected . . . I mean, two of her closest friends?'

'Sometimes we blot out the things we don't want to see. Who knows what goes through our minds sometimes? But it was over when she got back from Perth. She'd been out of the country for nearly two months. Marcus agreed to sublet her room during that time, because he was in transit himself, between flats. It was happening right under my nose and there was nothing I could do. I tried to have it out with Marcus, but he just put up the shutters, refused to discuss it.'

'And Julia?'

'Julia was the one who ended it. She was very confused, I remember. I think that for her, Marcus was a relief from boredom – it frustrated her being away from her boyfriend, Hayden, who's in Cambridge, and she wasn't one for being alone. She liked being the centre of attention.'

'That figures.' Maggie, without trying, was already

40

assembling a mental picture of Julia: the need to be noticed, the head-turning dress sense, the impulsive dash to marriage. Everyone, underneath, is insecure in some way, she thought absently. Not only nervous wrecks, like the train-spotter, but girls like Julia too, girls who on the face of it seem to have everything, who had no reason to lack confidence.

'Most of the involvement was on Marcus's side,' Christine went on, then chewing her lip as another customer arrived at the service point bearing books. Maggie hurried them through. The customer left and Christine continued. 'When things fell apart between them, he moved out. They had a terrible fight one night, screaming, throwing things. By that time a new flat had become available, anyway. As far as I could tell, Julia bottled out because of Hayden, she didn't want to ruin what she already had. Linda had only been back a few weeks when Julia announced she was leaving to marry. On the face of it, that was really the best arrangement for all concerned. It's hard to know *what* to think now, though.'

'Jesus.' This was beginning to make Maggie light-headed. 'Did I just stumble into a TV soap opera or what?'

'No.' Christine shrugged and laughed lightly. 'This is much too messy for prime time. It's all bitterness and recrimination and confusion. This is life.'

'And death,' Maggie said.

'Yes.' Christine swallowed. 'That too.'

7

By two in the morning, Maggie was still tossing and turning, unable to sleep. Through the open window she could hear the faint susurration of falling rain, a sound which normally lulled her. Now, it kept her awake. In its delicate pattern of drummings and whisperings, on the roof above her bed, in the streets below, she thought she heard voices, words trying to form themselves out of water. Which words though? Two words, she thought. The two words that tonight's *Evening Post* had been speculating about. The two words written on Julia Broderick's brow.

'I wish you could speak,' she said, burying her face in the pillow. 'I wish you could tell us what happened.'

She felt Julia's presence strongly tonight; no wonder she was restless. It was as though all this talk of her, all the stories the girls had to tell, were somehow preserving Julia, keeping her alive. Maggie had never known Julia Broderick in life – the artist's sketch on the poster, a photograph flashed on the TV news were all she had to go on – but now, too late, she felt she was beginning to.

Why had Julia allowed herself to become involved with Marcus in the first place? It wasn't that he was unappealing; in fairness quite the reverse. But even with Linda gone from the country, they'd been playing a risky game, a game of deceit that reflected badly on both of them. It was hurtful enough, she thought, that Ian had done what he'd done to her – the girl he'd been seeing for almost two months before she found out, Alison Grant, was not someone Maggie particularly knew well – but suppose it had been one of her friends? The knowledge of that would have broken her.

'Julia, if only you could explain,' she told her pillow, then lay for a while listening to the rain trying to speak. In the dark, with her eyes closed, she was able to summon up Julia's face, comparing it to her own. The similarity was striking if not exactly uncanny. Julia's features were perhaps rounder, warmer, her nose slightly smaller. It would have been easy to take them for sisters, though not necessarily twins.

Maggie's eyes opened in the dark. Why hadn't Marcus reacted the first time she'd met him? Even she was aware of the likeness; on first sighting the Missing poster, she'd glimpsed what she thought was herself. Regardless of how close Marcus had been to Julia, why hadn't he seen what the others had seen?

Sometimes we blot out the things we don't want to see, Christine had said. *Who knows what goes through our minds sometimes?*

The thoughts in her own mind were now so loud they were blotting out the sound of the rain. If she went on like this all night, she'd have nothing left for the morning; she'd have to drag herself to the library. Perhaps a glass of hot milk with honey would help; milk and honey were supposed to soothe you. She was reaching through the dark for the bedside light when she heard the telephone shrill in the next room.

Linda wouldn't answer it at this hour on principle, and Christine, who slept in a virtual coma, would never hear it. She slid out of bed, collected her dressing-gown and padded through to the living-room. The curtains were parted, the telephone glowed in a beacon of light from the street. Maggie lifted the receiver.

'Hello?'

It was exactly as before, as on the day she moved in. There was a presence on the line, a patient listener. She heard what she thought was a faint intake of breath.

'Hello?' she repeated. 'Who's there?' Gathering up the telephone from its place on the bookshelf, trailing the cord out behind her, she moved to the window, looking out through the rain-beaded glass. The houses opposite were blank, dark-windowed. The empty street below glistened in the rain. There was a telephone box down there, but, as far as she could tell, no one inside it.

'Julia,' a voice on the line said. She was certain that was what she'd just heard. The voice, a low whisper, could have been anyone's, female or male. 'Julia, I love you. I've been watching you. You're mine.'

'There's no Julia here,' she said firmly, doing her best to sound unaffected. But her stomach was knotting, her mind spinning. 'Wrong number.'

There was no reply. There was only the whirring silence, the suggestion of a voice that might and could speak but didn't, the patter of rain on the glass pane before her face. Then the familiar faint click as the caller hung up.

It took her several moments to return to herself.

The telephone purred in her hands. In a daze she replaced the receiver, fumbled her way to the nearest armchair, afraid of fainting if she didn't sit down immediately. Dragging her knees to her chin like a foetus she closed her eyes and felt herself sink.

'Maggie?' a voice said abruptly.

She opened her eyes with a start, registered daylight, the clock's hands spread-eagled above the fireplace, Linda standing over her, half-dressed in an oversized, white collarless shirt, and touched her hands to her throbbing temples.

'My God, you look like death,' Linda said.

'Careful. Unfortunate choice of words. What day is this?'

'A weekday, a work day like any other. Are you all right?'

Maggie shifted her position in the chair, wincing at the stiffness gripping her shoulders and neck. 'I – I think so. I must have fallen asleep here. Can't remember how or when. Wait a minute.' She tried to sit up. The telephone lay on the floor beside the chair. 'Yes, yes I can. There was a call, a very late call. Someone asking for Julia. They seemed to think . . .'

'Yes?' Linda stiffened. 'What happened?'

'I got scared. They spoke to me as if they thought *I* was Julia. They said things . . .'

Linda frowned. 'You're being incredibly vague, Mags. What did they say?'

'Just a few words. I love you, you're mine, something like that. And for a moment I thought – hell, I don't know what I thought.'

'You're still disorientated. Wait right there and I'll

bring you a coffee with enough caffeine to kill a horse.'
She ran to the kitchen.

Maggie brightened. It was almost impossible now,
with the morning light streaming into the flat, to
explain last night, her momentary terror, to Linda or
even herself. The voice on the phone had called her
Julia: so what? Suppose it was someone who hadn't
yet heard what had happened? Someone, admittedly,
who'd been living out of the country or with his or
her head firmly buried in the sand for the past
week.

'Sounds like another crank call,' Linda said, returning with strong black coffee. 'Everyone gets them. It
happens in phases. There's nothing to worry about.'

'Didn't you say you had a spate of these calls while
Julia was here?'

'That's right. I answered a few myself. I mean, I
understand how some people let that kind of thing get
to them, but basically what you're dealing with is some
inadequate jerk on the line, someone without the bottle
to speak up for themselves, who'd jump a mile if you
ever confronted them in the street.'

'And that's it? You don't think whoever it is could
be dangerous?'

'If they were really worth losing sleep over, they
wouldn't be wasting our time or theirs with mere
phone calls, is my bet.'

'But Julia lost sleep over them, didn't she?'

'I wouldn't have said it was as bad as all that. She
became preoccupied and upset at one point. She came
out of it later on, but for a time she was convinced that
someone was watching or following her.'

'Watching her?' But that was what the voice had

told Maggie last night; or had she dreamt that part? 'Where did she get that idea?'

Linda reclined on the sofa opposite Maggie, began studiously backcombing her hair. 'There was a kid,' she said, 'a student I think, who she'd met once or twice at the Uni. She described him as nervous and edgy, but somehow he found the courage to ask her out, even called here in person to see her one night. Julia asked me to tell him she wasn't home, and he never showed his face again. Later on, she claimed she kept seeing him here, there and everywhere, in the supermarket, the book shops, in Principles and Russell and Bromley. As far as Julia was concerned, the boy was infatuated.'

'Did you believe her?'

'Why shouldn't I?'

'I don't know. I suppose I wondered whether she might have seen ghosts where there weren't any.'

'Well, one ghost or another sent her packing to the morgue in a hurry.' Linda looked briefly indignant. Then she returned to her hair. 'I'm sorry. You have a point. Julia always did want drama – capital D – in her life, and I have to admit it crossed my mind that she was attention-seeking. You know, that the phone calls *were* cranks but she was reading a whole lot more into them, that the boy was a fantasy figure. I thought all those things. But *someone* got to her, didn't they? Someone did that to her. It wasn't entirely her imagination.'

Maggie sipped her coffee in silence for a time. The caffeine, besides waking her, seemed to be prickling her nerves again. 'This student,' she said. 'Did you know him?'

47

'Only really by sight. Something of a misfit, I would've said. He was kind of grungy and unkempt, a little left-field for my taste. And Julia's.' She gave a wry smile. 'No doubt Chris would take him to her heart. She goes for those downbeat types.'

'I heard that,' Christine said, flouncing in from her room. Her thick dark hair was matted across her face, like a sheepdog's fringe. She was wearing a huge, tent-like Nirvana T-shirt which drooped to her knees. 'Not interrupting you, I hope.'

'I thought you could sleep through Armageddon,' Maggie said.

'So I can. But when I'm being talked about I develop antennae. Is there any more of that coffee?' She slammed her way into the kitchen, returning seconds later, bearing a steaming mug. Swiping hair from her eyes, she sank into the sofa beside Linda. 'As you were,' she said, waving one hand like an orchestral conducter. 'You know I can't stand to miss anything.'

'We were talking about the student,' Maggie said. 'The one that came up to see Julia that time.'

'Oh, him. Yes, I know who you mean.' To Linda she said, 'What gives you the idea I'd take *him* to my heart?'

'Don't you think,' Maggie said after an interval, 'it's time you two talked to the police again about Julia?'

Linda nodded. 'I've been thinking that too. Not that I'd know what to tell them.'

'What you've told me already would make a pretty good start.' She met Christine's gaze as she added, 'There must be a lot about Julia they don't know yet. For instance, who was the guy she said was following her? Do you remember his name?'

48

'I'm not sure he ever gave it, did he?' Christine was staring at Linda for a clue that never came. Slowly, a look of amusement crept over her, and she gave a pleasurable shiver. 'But I do remember what Julia once called him. It cracked me up, really it did, because it seemed so appropriate. The train-spotter, she called him.'

'Right.' Linda blinked, but didn't quite manage a smile. 'The train-spotter.'

'What?' Maggie practically leapt from her seat. Coffee spilt from her cup, splashing the carpet. '*What was that?*'

Christine stared back at her, bewildered. 'Something I said?' she asked meekly.

8

Maggie was now looking forward to the weekend, which she planned to spend with her parents. The first days at the flat had been nothing if not dramatic – dramatic with a capital D, as Linda might have put it – and now she craved normality, if only for an evening, or a lazy Sunday morning reading the newspapers. She needed time to clear her head of the billion dark details crowding in on her.

During Friday afternoon lunch-break she took a swift walk to Safeway's in the city centre, filling her basket with pasta and garlic bread and shitaki mushrooms for the evening blow-out. She was barely through the check-out when she saw Ian standing in the pedestrian precinct beyond the doors.

He couldn't be waiting for her, could he? She hoped not, even though he was looking her way, since she still had nothing to say to him: her first week of independence had been difficult, but at least it had helped her flush him out of her system. In part she'd wanted to move for that reason alone. Being at home gave her too much time to think, to stew in her own juices. As she passed through the check-out, shovelling change into her purse and provisions into a plastic bag, Ian hurried inside.

Before she could recoil he'd kissed her cheek, seized her bag from the counter. 'I was passing and I saw you in the line,' he said, smiling. 'Let me help you with that.'

'Thanks. I can manage.'

He stopped for a moment to look at her, taking her in as if for the first time. 'Long time no see, Mags. You look great. You haven't changed one iota, I'm glad to say.'

'Thank you. I'm surprised to see you.'

'Just one of those things. Call it fate. Which way are you going?'

'Back towards the wharf. I work in the branch library near there.'

'So you're working now.'

'As of last week. It's just the first rung of the ladder, but it suits me. And you?'

'Still doing those resits, which is a drag, but a necessary drag. Oh, and I finally started editing the school magazine, I always wanted to do that.'

'I know. Sounds great.' As they paused to window-gaze outside the Sweater Shop, she suppressed a slight flutter of emotion. She wasn't as angry at Ian as she'd expected to be; she could only think of times when they'd shopped here before, pausing and browsing, hand in hand, and of evenings when he'd talked of his plans for the magazine, how he'd transform it if they ever gave him the chance.

'Do you have any plans, apart from getting back to work?' he asked.

She faltered. 'I have half an hour to play with.'

'Time for a coffee? I'm buying.'

It would have been easy to say no if he'd suggested

it on the telephone. As long as she didn't have to see his face, his boyish expectant face, she was strong. On balance, he didn't deserve her time; it wasn't so long ago that he'd excused himself from meeting her after school only to spend his time with Alison, as she later discovered. But this was only a coffee, for crying out loud. What was she afraid of?

'All right,' she said.

They found seats in Stefano's, a basement wine bar just a short walk away. Ian brought coffees to the table. 'You're not at home any more, I hear,' he said matter-of-factly.

'How do you know?'

'I called last night, had a bit of a chat with your dad. He gave me your new number, although he was a little reluctant and I had to plead in the end. I would've been getting in touch soon, which is why seeing you like this is so weird.' He ran his fingers back through his thick sandy hair. 'Running into you like this, I mean. It was meant to be.'

'I wouldn't read too much into it,' Maggie said flatly.

Ian nodded, his gaze drifting away. She knew him well enough by now to know there were things he was only just holding back from saying. 'How's the new place?' he asked.

'Good question. The flat itself, and my flatmates, are terrific. But the whole week's been an endurance test.'

'How so?'

'The girl who lived there before me, the girl whose room I've taken, was Julia Broderick. Maybe you heard –'

'I know,' he said, cutting her short. 'I've been following the story. What a nightmare.' He fell silent for a moment or two, then looked at her sharply. 'I saw her photograph in the newspapers. And I couldn't believe my eyes. I mean, Jesus, Maggie –'

'Yes. I know. I know all about it. Don't I just!'

'The idea of you taking her place – you know, taking her room and all. It's such a coincidence, don't you think?'

'I wish I believed in coincidence.'

Ian was searching her face for an explanation. 'Meaning what, exactly?'

'Nothing. I didn't mean anything by it.' But perhaps, in a way, she did, if she only had the nerve to admit it. Perhaps that was why her nights had been restless just lately. The last week had been full of so-called coincidences: the poster, the phone calls, her passing resemblance to the girl she'd replaced. Surely there came a point where coincidence stopped and became something far more sinister.

'Is it bothering you, being here with me?' Ian asked. 'You're a little uneasy.'

'Who wouldn't be after this week? No, Ian.' She flashed a smile, intending to reassure him. 'It's good to see you again. Easier than I thought it would be.'

He seemed to relax at last. 'I was thinking so too. I mean, apart from the dreadful stuff that's happening around you, you look terrific. In a way you've never looked better.' From habit he reached for her across the table, then seemed to think better of it and withdrew his hand. 'The truth is, I've been wondering about you. Whether or not you . . .' He broke off, dry-lipped.

'I'm not sure I want to hear this,' she said. She sensed what was coming; had sensed it the moment she'd laid eyes on him at the check-out. She glanced at her watch. 'I have to fly.'

'Please. Not yet. There's something I have to tell you.'

'Just as I figured. Another time perhaps, when I'm not in a hurry.' She stood and began edging from the table.

Before she'd taken two steps, Ian seized her wrist, seized it so hard her watch-strap dug into her skin. 'This won't wait,' he said. 'It's clear in my mind now. I've been figuring out exactly how to put this.'

'Ah. You've been rehearsing your lines.'

'Sit down again, will you? Just for a minute.'

'First, let go of my wrist.' When he relented, she drew a chair back from the table, positioning it a few feet away out of arm's reach, and slid into it. 'Well?' she said.

'I'm sorry,' he said. 'About everything that happened before. It was such a dumb thing, such a mess.'

'Yes, it was. *Your* mess.'

'I admit, I lost my head, didn't give a thought to anyone else. Yes, Alison did sweep me off my feet, but I wouldn't blame her for everything. I behaved like a bastard.'

'Yes, you did.'

'But it's over now. And I want ... what I really want ...' he began, then faltered. 'Maggie, I don't know how to say this.'

'Then don't bother. Let me use my imagination.'

'I want you back.'

She had seen that one coming; she shouldn't have

stayed long enough to hear it. It had been a mistake to come here in the first place. Suddenly there was a tightness in her throat and a heat in her eyes like a warning of tears she couldn't prevent. She mustn't let herself go though, not now, not like this.

'Do you think you can switch me on and off to suit yourself?' she said. 'Let me tell you something, Ian: it just isn't done to pick people up and put them down as you please.'

'I don't want you seeing anyone else.'

'Since when were we engaged? It's no business of yours who I choose to see.'

'Maggie. Let's talk about this,' he pleaded. He was painfully near to tears himself now.

'We *are* talking, but there's nothing more to say. You were totally out of line, Ian. End of story. I'd like you to think about that before you see me again. Now excuse me.'

There was a lull – six or eight beats of the pulse in her throat – as she picked up her groceries and made for the door. As she reached it, he came back at her, his voice at once cold, hard, transformed. 'You'll be sorry,' he said.

'I'll – what? What's that supposed to mean?'

'You'll regret this mistake, Maggie, believe me.'

'Well, Ian, I've got news for you. The mistake was all yours. Goodbye.'

She was breathless when she reached the top of the steps leading up from the wine bar. Outside, the precinct vibrated with shoppers mummified in warm coats and scarves, their collars upturned against the biting air. Shop windows glittered with early Christmas displays. The sight of their reds, greens and silvers, so striking a contrast to the grey October day, would normally have lifted her spirits. Instead she was shaking, her nerve-ends charged with static. How could she let Ian upset her like this, especially after she'd promised herself he never would again? Tightening her grip on the shopping bags, she started up the precinct in a trance, not caring where she was going. As she went, Ian's last words filled her mind like a fog, crowding everything else out.

You'll be sorry . . . You'll regret this mistake, believe me . . .

It wasn't what he'd said, but the way that he'd said it. Had he meant to threaten her, or had it just come out that way? Lost in thought, she didn't even notice the figure in a shop doorway away to her left – a figure wearing an army jacket, faded jeans and old sneakers – duck quickly inside out of sight as she passed.

9

The bus shuddered along Fitzroy Street, spinning Maggie towards the driver the instant she vacated her seat. As she fumbled for balance, grasping one of the metal posts near the front with her free hand, she found herself face to face with Julia Broderick.

That was her first impression, but the woman in the grey raincoat with the tweaked-up collar was actually several years older than Julia, her looks pointed up with cosmetics. The lank blonde hair, sharp grey eyes and lipsticked gash of a mouth were only a pale shadow of Julia's features. The woman frowned, perhaps because Maggie was staring, and seemed on the verge of speaking when the bus jolted again and the doors slapped open at the stop.

You're beginning to see her in your sleep, in your *soup*, Maggie thought, watching the bus out of sight before crossing the street. Even the new police posters of Julia with their pleading notices – DO YOU HAVE INFORMATION WHICH WILL HELP FIND THIS GIRL'S KILLER? – seemed to scream at her from every shop window she passed. But since when did Julia wear blood-red lipstick? It really wasn't her style.

Not that she could be certain about what was or

wasn't her style – but she *was* developing a feel for the kind of girl Julia must've been. After all, Linda and Christine had painted such a vivid picture of her during the week, Maggie felt she was coming to know her as well as herself. And perhaps Julia *had* worn garish red lipstick for her last night on earth, if only for shock value.

Maggie turned on to Calderwood Grove, switching her overnight bag from hand to hand. Keep her out of your mind, she told herself sternly. At least for now. That's why you're here for the weekend, isn't it, to get her out from under your skin? But footsteps close behind her, as she reached her parents' drive, still made her flinch, half-expecting – insanely – to see Julia when she swung around to see who was there. 'Maggie, what's *wrong* with you?' she muttered, loudly enough to bring a long, wary glare from a bald-headed man who was crossing the street to his car.

The house was warm and aromatic, the garlicky smell of Saturday lunch drifting along the hall to welcome her as she hung up her jacket. In the kitchen, her mother clattered plates and pans, opened and closed the oven door like an automaton. Her father sat at the table, a copy of the *Evening Post*'s first edition spread out before him. As Maggie entered, he peered above the thick marbled frames of his glasses, blowing a kiss. She pecked his cheek as she reached for a chair.

'Something smells good,' she said.

'House speciality,' her mother said proudly. 'You must miss your old mum's home cooking now you're gone, just tell me you don't.'

'Bribery will get you nowhere.'

Her mother smiled, but there was an air of acceptance about her, Maggie thought, as if she'd finally realized pleading wouldn't help. 'Well, then, how was your journey?' Now she hovered over the table, a steaming casserole dish balanced between her oven-gloved hands.

'Journey?' Maggie tried not to laugh. 'Mum, the bus ride takes fifteen minutes.'

'You might as well be a hundred miles away as far as she's concerned,' Maggie's father said, grinning. 'She reckons she's lost you for good.'

'Nonsense.' Her mother twitched her nose as if the chicken chasseur didn't meet her expectations. 'I'm concerned, that's all. What kind of mother would I be if I weren't? I suppose everything's just fine where she is, and the streets are well lit and safe.'

'Everything *is* fine, really it is,' Maggie tried to assure her. 'It's an up-and-coming area. Better than I'd hoped for, and I wouldn't have been able to afford living there without sharing. Linda and Christine are like sisters to me . . .' She stopped herself there. Perhaps she shouldn't make it sound too sensational, or her enthusiasm might seem like a snub. Besides, there were things she wouldn't dare mention: there *was* a down-side, and since the phone calls began she really hadn't felt safe. 'Also, it's close to work, practically walking distance,' she added brightly.

'Good. Very good.'

Her father said nothing, made meticulous folds in his newspaper as he set it aside. A half-concealed headline said POLICE INVEST, which Maggie imagined referred to the Julia Broderick case. 'Can I see that?' she asked, but her mother was already serving.

'As soon as we've finished. First eat, then read. As

long as you're under my roof –' Her mother smiled faintly. '– you'll respect the house rules.'

One of which was to clear the dishes immediately after each meal. Maggie shared the chore with her father, the sight of whom in squeaking yellow gloves and floral pinafore always gave her a fit of the giggles.

'Something wrong?' he asked quietly as soon as they were alone.

Maggie shrugged. Thank God for him; if only her mother were so laid back, so willing to take everything in her stride. 'I wish I could talk to her about this,' she said. 'She seems so preoccupied. She's taking it badly, isn't she?'

'Taking what badly?'

'You know. My moving out.'

'She's missing you,' he said without looking at her. 'You know you'll be able to talk to her properly as soon as everything's settled.'

'But she's had a whole week. How long will she need?'

'Just a while longer. You'll see.'

'She really is worried, Dad, isn't she?'

'Worried?' He seemed to be stalling, rewashing a perfectly clean plate for the second or third time. 'She has nothing to worry *about*, does she?'

'Maybe she thinks she does.'

The splash of water, the clink of plates filled the silence between them for a moment. Then he said, 'She worries about the same things every parent does. A young woman, living alone –'

'Not alone, Dad. Sharing with two others, remember.'

'I know. In a respectable part of town. All well and good. But you have to consider things from *her* point of view . . .'

'What are you getting at? This sounds like *your* point of view, not hers.'

'It's hers and mine, both. Be careful, that's all I'm saying.'

Maggie regarded him blankly. Yes, of course she understood what he meant; but to hear this from her father, who never ever fretted about anything, who always appeared so untroubled, surprised her.

'What brought this on?' she asked. 'This sudden concern?'

'You read the newspapers. You know well enough what everyone's talking about.'

Don't I just, Maggie thought, stacking dried dishes. 'I'm careful about the company I keep,' she said defensively. 'And I do have a head on my shoulders. I'm not bloody stupid.'

'Of course you're not stupid. All the same, you're spending your time with new people now, you're moving in different circles. And sometimes, Maggie, people can appear to be what they're not. Understand?'

She thought that she did, but at first she didn't reply. Plates and knives fluttered in her grasp as she wiped and set them aside. He was talking about people like – well, people like Marcus, perhaps. Or the train-spotter, with his shifty gaze and his books about serial killers. Or even people like Ian, who had virtually threatened her yesterday. He's talking about what's under the surface, she thought, as her father lifted a razor-sharp cook's knife from the grey soapy water; the things other people conceal from us, the things we can't see and don't even suspect until it's too late.

'I hear you,' she said.

By four o'clock the light was fading. While her parents lolled in front of the TV, she scanned the *Evening Post*. The story told her nothing she didn't already know, though another passing reference to the words inscribed on Julia's brow gave her the jitters, especially as the report still failed to reveal what the message was. When the local TV news began, she hurried from the lounge, afraid of sitting through yet another report on the murder while her parents were present. She couldn't abide the thought of them scrutinizing her face for clues while the story unfolded.

A quick blast of negative ions under the shower calmed her, at least for a time. If you're not careful, she told herself, dressing in jeans and an oversized grey sweatshirt, you're going to wind up *thinking* like Julia, suspicious of every phone call, jumping at shadows.

But perhaps, in a way, she *should* be thinking like Julia. Perhaps there was a reason she'd landed where she had, in Julia's shoes – Julia's pumps – and it wasn't by chance, it couldn't be. She belonged where circumstance had put her. And she now had a perfect opportunity to uncover the truth; to learn what no one else could. And why?

'What kind of nonsense is this?' she said aloud, scolding herself. 'What's going on in your *head*, Mags?'

She didn't want to face it yet, but it was becoming more obvious by the day, and it terrified her. She straightened the towels on their heated rail, dumped her used clothes in the linen basket, checked her reflection in the mirror before leaving the bathroom.

As she did, the telephone rang down in the hall. She hesitated half-way downstairs while her father padded from the lounge to answer it. For one dreadful moment she imagined the call wouldn't be for herself but for Julia, that a soft male voice would whisper, 'I love you' as her father passed her the receiver. But he was smiling and clutching the phone to his chest.

'Christine for you,' he said.

She sat on the stairs, four steps from the bottom, the telephone cable trailing around the rail to her ankles. 'So there you are,' Christine said. P.J. Harvey screamed in the background. 'Just checking up on you. How's everything?'

'Oh, fine. I just feel a little –'

'I know, you sound drained. I told you a life of debauchery would get you nowhere. Are they feeding you properly?'

Maggie laughed. 'You sound like my mother.'

'Does your mother worry about stuff like that too? Aren't mums marvellous?' Christine drew a short breath before going on. 'Maggie, I hope I'm not interrupting anything.'

'No, I just stepped out of the shower. I'm slobbing around. Is everything OK?'

'As OK as can be. I wouldn't have called, but there was something I wanted – we wanted to discuss with you.'

'Go ahead.'

'Well, we finally did what you said we should do, and I stopped in with Linda at the police station today. Told them everything we could.'

'Good. I knew it was the right thing to do. Did you talk about Julia and Marcus?'

'Yes, even that. It was all kind of hard on Linda, though; it's something she's never discussed openly with me, even though she'd had it all out with Marcus, but you can't withhold information like that, can you? You can either tell everything or nothing. We thrashed it all out beforehand, of course. It wasn't something I wanted to force her into doing.'

'Sure.' Maggie nodded, as if Christine could see her. 'How is she now?'

'Very down, as you'd imagine. She's been keeping to her room since we got back.' Christine lowered her voice very slightly. 'It's hitting her worse now than at first. I think she's been holding all this inside herself.'

It was almost impossible to know what to say, what reassurances to give. 'Just send her my love,' Maggie said. 'Tell her I'm thinking of her.'

'I will. She'll appreciate that.' Another pause. 'There was something else, though.'

'About Julia?'

'Yes. I don't know quite how to put this. It's just a suggestion; don't pay any attention to it if you don't want to. Don't feel obligated.'

'I'm riveted already. What's happening?'

'At the police station we gave our report to one of the officers, a desk sergeant called Morrison. Kind of cute, if you ask me, but that's off the point. When we'd finished, he happened to mention they were looking for someone who fitted Julia's description. They're planning to reconstruct what happened to her that night; to shoot the whole thing on video or film.'

'Ah.' Maggie sensed her mouth running dry. 'I think I can guess where this is leading.' It was where

64

the whole bizarre week, and today in particular, had been leading her.

'Don't worry,' Christine said. 'We didn't even mention your name. We thought that the least we could do would be to check with you first.'

10

Now she was truly becoming like Julia. It wasn't the sheer, black, sleeveless dress she had on – a dress which she'd picked up on sale at Principles and which clung to her thighs like a second skin – so much as the make-up that made all the difference. As she studied herself in the dresser's mirror, adding a trace of lipstick, a hint of eyeliner, she sensed the others holding their breath.

'My God,' Christine said.

'I know,' Linda added, her voice a nervous murmur.

This wasn't Julia's usual style, Maggie was certain. Julia hadn't needed cosmetics to point up her natural assets, but even she would have been lost in this outfit without them. Now she recapped the lipstick and checked her reflection critically. There was no doubt about it; in the course of half an hour she'd left herself behind and moved on, she'd seen her face slowly transform itself into Julia's. If your folks could see you now, she thought, if they had any idea what you're planning, they'd *really* have something to fret about.

'It's remarkable,' Linda said, holding Maggie's gaze in the mirror. 'There was a likeness before, but this . . .'

'Don't forget the hair,' Christine said. 'She would've

worn it loose with this dress, not tied back, the way you've got it.'

Without hesitation, Maggie removed the band from her hair, returning it to the dresser's clutter. Then she picked up the bottle of Anaïs Anaïs Linda had brought in, sprayed a little on her wrists, smeared a little between her breasts. The scent wouldn't make any difference to what the camera crew captured on tape, but it helped her feel more secure in the role. She had done all the preparation she could.

'Well? What's the verdict?' Maggie half-turned towards them.

'The first word that springs to mind is scary,' Christine said. She was shaking her head, open-mouthed.

'Truly scary.' Linda uttered a mirthless laugh.

'Well, thanks very much. That's guaranteed to make me feel just great.'

'You know what we're saying,' Christine said. 'You're a picture, of course you are. But imagine how it feels to see you like this. If only I had a glitzy photo of Julia to show you, you'd flip. You *are* her.'

'Well, I'm certainly beginning to feel less like *me*.' Maggie glanced down at her bare white feet with their varnished toenails which Christine had insisted on painting. Perhaps that was taking things too far, but events had somehow swept her away today, and no detail had seemed too outlandish. The camera unit had arrived, as had the police, who were to supervise the reconstruction. They were waiting out in the lounge even now.

'Are you ready?' Linda asked.

'I think so. But nerve-racked.'

Together they left the room. A detective Maggie

recognized from last week's TV news occupied one of the chairs in the lounge. Behind him, a second plain-clothes officer gazed from the misty window at the darkening sky. The cameraman and sound recordist were still rigging lights, angling the powerful lamps towards the ceiling. A third member of the crew, a narrow-faced, bearded man, stood rifling pages of a clipboard he was holding. The others stopped to look up from their work as Maggie entered, and for a moment she felt at a loss, embarrassed by so much attention.

'This is nothing compared to what you'll feel when it's broadcast,' D.I. Penhaligon said, rising from the armchair to take her hand. 'Just relax, if you can in this heat.' The lights had turned the lounge into a sauna. A single bead of condensation trickled down the wall above the fireplace. 'Better sit down until the boys give you the nod.'

'How long will this take, do you think?'

'Not long, once we're set up,' the bearded man, who Maggie assumed was the director, told her. 'We only need a couple of shots here.'

Linda and Christine had agreed, without much ca-joling, to play themselves in the reconstruction. Well, if *I* have to do it, Maggie had told them, *you* don't even have a choice. In Linda's case, this would pro-vide her first dramatic role outside college: her TV debut might have been cause for celebration if the circumstances had been any different, any less traumatic.

In any case, she and Christine were only required for one brief scene inside the flat, when Julia had dropped by, around seven, that Thursday evening. As far as Linda and Christine were concerned, there had been no hard feelings at her leaving so quickly. She was a friend and they wished her the very best. Over coffee Julia described how she'd sent her belongings to Hayden in Cambridge and moved temporarily into a bedsit near Leeds University. She had already quit her course, and would be leaving town at the weekend. When Julia finally excused herself and left, Linda had been preparing dinner at the kitchen stove – 'A little more spaghetti on the wall for authenticity,' Maggie quipped – while Christine sprawled on the sofa, programming tracks on the CD remote.

Much to Maggie's relief, she wasn't required to act; only to go through the motions of being Julia. 'It isn't supposed to be drama,' D.I. Penhaligon assured her. 'All we're hoping for is to strike a chord with some viewer out there; someone who hasn't come forward yet, probably because they don't even realize they crossed paths with Julia that night. Perhaps this will jog their memory.'

When the camera unit were ready, Maggie was invited to breeze about the lounge, collecting her bag from the floor, popping her head round the kitchen door to say goodbye to Linda. Then, before leaving, she picked up the phone and dialled. Regardless of what Penhaligon had told her, she felt uncomfortably close to acting, having to force herself not to look at the camera.

On the sofa, Christine watched while Maggie/Julia talked on the phone. The CD selection was playing now, and Julia's words were almost inaudible. The call was a detail she'd overlooked until Saturday at the police station, a detail which hadn't meant anything to her before then. But the police seemed to feel it could be significant.

Who had she called before leaving? Perhaps Hayden in Cambridge, though Hayden's statement to the police didn't confirm this. Then perhaps she was speaking to someone she intended to meet that evening. Or simply ordering a taxi. The police wanted anyone who might have spoken to her between eight and eight-thirty to volunteer the fact.

Now the director called for a close-up of Christine shifting on the sofa, looking across towards Maggie/Julia. This was followed by a shot, from Christine's point of view, of Maggie/Julia shielding the receiver with both hands while talking into it, facing the window. Christine lowered the volume on the stereo slightly. A low burring filled Maggie's ear as she gripped the phone. It was a blank dialling tone, but through it she half-imagined a whispering voice telling her: Julia, I love you, you're mine, I –

Now D.I. Penhaligon turned to Christine. 'How did Julia appear to you after she'd finished the call? Happy? Distraught? Had it been an emotional call, would you say?'

Christine shook her head. 'She looked impassive, the way Maggie played it just now. She smiled when she saw me watching her, but the smile didn't last. That's how I remember it, anyway. Then she told me she'd see me again before she left town. She didn't actually speak the words out loud but mouthed them over the music. I'm fairly sure that's what she meant. She set off right after that.' She glanced forlornly at Linda, wringing her hands. 'And the rest, as they say, is history.'

'We've covered everything we need here,' Penhaligon told the director, who nodded as if well aware of the fact. The cameraman was already packing up his camera, while the soundman uncoupled the lights.

A script, of a kind, had been cobbled together for the reconstruction. It had been compiled, Penhaligon explained as they trooped downstairs and outdoors, from the database the police had built up during their inquiries. A number of witnesses had sighted Julia – at least someone fitting her description – in several locations across the city that night.

'We know she couldn't have been in all of those places at once,' the detective said, 'but three people in Little Rico's coffee bar saw her there around nine o'clock, and another two spotted her getting into a car outside a nightclub called V about three hours later. It's very likely that she went to both places. The nightclub's a five-minute walk from Rico's.' He held open the rear door of his BMW while the girls piled inside, shuddering from the cold. 'We'll see you there,' he called vaguely as the camera crew reached their van. Then he climbed in behind the wheel.

The other plain-clothes detective took the passenger seat, turning towards the girls while Penhaligon drove. 'Did you see Julia take her coat when she left?' he asked Christine.

She needed to consider for a moment or two. 'No, but if she took it from the hook inside the entrance to the flat I wouldn't have been able to. It's in an alcove out of sight from the lounge. In any case, I was fussing about with the remote.' She hugged herself briefly for warmth, then turned to Linda. 'You let her in when she arrived, didn't you? Was she wearing a coat then?'

Linda shrugged. 'I think so. She must've been.'

'It was a night like tonight – deadly freezing. She wouldn't have gone without one, would she? I know you see masochists wandering round the city in shirt-sleeves at all times of year, but she wasn't like that. She looked after herself.'

'What do your witnesses say?' Maggie asked.

'There's some confusion there. Some say she wore a jacket, some remember only the dress.' Penhaligon slowed for the lights on Lower Briggate. The streets were clogging with rush-hour traffic, flaring with green and red neon from the windows of pizza restaurants. Crowds of pedestrians lined up at bus-stops, milled about the doorways of shops as the shutters came down. 'We've tried to assemble a picture of events that makes sense to *us*, and that's what we're asking you to act out. It's very likely that Julia left the coat somewhere.'

'But someone would have found it,' Linda said. 'Wouldn't they have reported it?'

'Not if they were homeless and freezing,' D.I. Penhaligon's assistant said. 'Half our problem is the information that never gets volunteered because some of the people we'd like to come forward – potentially key witnesses – have something to hide. Perhaps someone stole the coat.'

'Where are we heading?' Maggie asked, staring from the window at a raggedy tramp rooting through an unemptied litter bin half-way up Briggate.

'The coffee bar first. Then the night-club,' Penhaligon said. 'I hope you can handle a late night, which is what this could easily become. I'll straighten things out with your employers tomorrow, if you need me to.'

'Thanks.'

The traffic was moving again, but now they were slowing, drawing to the kerb near the Victoria Quarter, an arcade of designer shops. Penhaligon waited until the camera crew's van pulled up behind them before jumping out.

'Stay here,' he told the girls. 'You may as well keep warm until everything's ready inside.' The other detective followed Penhaligon into the arcade.

'You're very quiet,' Christine said presently. 'You've hardly muttered a word in the last hour.'

At first Maggie thought Christine meant her, but she was talking to Linda.

'I don't know,' Linda said. 'I've been like this ever since the weekend. I've had to face a few unpleasant home truths since telling the story to that cop.'

'What home truths?' Christine asked.

'Well, for instance, about Marcus.' Linda glanced quickly at Maggie, then gave her hand a firm squeeze. 'I'm sorry I didn't come clean to you about it before – Julia and Marcus, I mean. I suppose it's something I felt I could sweep under the carpet, but it keeps coming back at me.' She paused, staring deep inside the arcade, though there was little to see, since most of the shops and boutiques had now doused their lights. 'Still, at least she didn't head out to see Marcus that night – it was over between them; had been for weeks. But seeing this . . . this action replay . . . brings it all to the surface again. It's kind of hard on me.'

Christine said, 'There's something I never asked you before, because the timing never seemed right. How do you *know* she didn't see Marcus after she left us?'

In the half-light that bathed the space inside the car, Maggie sensed Linda flinch. 'Because *I* was at Marcus's that night,' she said coolly. 'I went to his place right after dinner.'

There was a brief, stony lull. Then Maggie felt something dig sharply into her side: Christine's elbow. It might have been unintentional, but she didn't think so. For one thing, Christine didn't apologize, and for another, she'd become almost unnaturally silent, as if holding her breath in shocked disbelief.

Seconds later the director appeared at the window, beckoning Maggie to join him. Whether or not Christine had been trying to tell her something, she was glad when the moment passed and she was back in the bracing night air again. Whatever was going on here wasn't something she dared to think about yet.

11

The coffee bar was scarcely large enough to house ten people, let alone the film unit's equipment and lights. The décor sparkled with polished mahogany and brass hand- and foot-rails at the counter and along the walls, where customers perched on high, precarious-looking stools. Ambient techno music played softly through speakers half-hidden by plants. When Maggie arrived at the entrance, the half dozen young people already inside turned to stare as if a ghost had just joined them. They'd seen her image on the TV, of course, and in the newspapers too – Julia's image, not hers.

Just remember who you are, she reminded herself. They might well be seeing Julia Broderick, but they're looking at *you*. Maggie hesitated at the doorway, studying her pale frozen fingers.

Once the lights had been rigged and the camera adjusted on its tripod, she was invited to enter the bar, take a stool at the counter and order a coffee. Four or five statements the police had taken agreed that a striking young woman had whiled away half an hour here, occasionally glancing at her watch or out of the window. Some said she'd removed a light-coloured jacket or raincoat as she entered, slinging it over the back of her stool before sitting. Others remembered only the dress. D.I. Penhaligon asked Maggie to enter wearing a coat.

Maggie checked her watch while the camera rolled. She glanced out the window, just as Julia had. She was nervous, edgy. Julia must have felt like this, sitting here. Presumably she'd been waiting for someone, but who? Surely not Marcus; but Maggie still felt the pressure of Christine's elbow in her ribs, as though Christine had been trying to tell her something without upsetting Linda.

Julia, she thought, what *did* happen to you that night? Who were you meeting, and whose was the last face you ever saw? You've *got* to tell me, she thought, because one way or another I'm going to find out. I don't *want* to, I didn't *ask* to become involved, but here I am, look at me: I'm becoming like you and there's no turning back.

Seconds later someone called cut, breaking her reverie. For a moment she lingered at the bar, idly stirring her cappuccino until its dusting of chocolate powder dissolved. A couple of customers were still gawking. She could feel their eyes on her back like faint prickles of heat. One man, wearing a spotless, blue linen suit with a white shirt and red Paisley tie, looked away sharply as she spun round on her stool to meet his stare. In fact, he hadn't been staring *at* her so much as into her, through her. A dark, square-jawed type, handsome as a model in *Esquire*, his chic Mediterranean looks wouldn't have been out of place in a swish, well-heeled nightclub like V.

Not your type, Maggie told herself firmly. He may be a hunk but not *your* kind of hunk. More importantly, not Julia's type either. Julia hadn't fallen for the grungy train-spotter, but she still preferred casual, downbeat types, at least if Marcus was anything to go by. She wondered absently whether the girls had ever met Hayden, and if they had, what he was like. She imagined an arty older man, slightly dishevelled and distracted.

Now the director was calling the crew to train their camera and lights on the hunk in the suit. They required one brief shot of him looking at Julia, before moving on.

'He didn't just happen to be here,' Penhaligon's assistant told her. 'His name is Dave Sessions. We invited him to take part because he was here the night Julia came in.'

It took no more than ten minutes before the filming was completed. Maggie followed Penhaligon towards the door, where Christine and Linda waited, while the crew repacked their equipment. Just as she passed the stool where Dave Sessions was sitting, the hunk stood up, touching her arm. Maggie swallowed hard.

'I'm sorry,' he said. 'I startled you.' His soft brown eyes held hers for an instant before he looked down. 'And I was staring.'

'Yes, you were.'

'It's just that Julia Broderick made quite an impression on me when she walked into this place. And this – it's a little like seeing her again.'

Maggie glanced at the doorway. Christine, predictably, was grinning, eyes wide as saucers. She felt her cheeks burning. 'Let's say a little make-up goes a long way,' she said.

'No kidding. If I . . .' He was fumbling; not as cool

and collected as he'd seemed from a distance. 'Well, perhaps you'd better get going. I'm keeping you.'

She checked the doorway again. The others were turning away up the arcade now. The cameraman dodged past her, thumping his case against the door-jamb as he squeezed out of the coffee bar. Dave Sessions spoke in a confidential whisper she could barely hear above the faint clatter of crockery.

'Were you a friend of Julia's?' he asked. 'I know the police sometimes invite friends to do what you're doing.'

'We never met. I'm sharing a place with two girls who were friends of hers.'

'Ah. It must be a very stressful time for you all.'

'You could say that.'

'If there's anything I can do . . .'

'I'm sure you've been a great help to the police just by being here.'

'That's not what I meant. I meant for you.' She could've sworn that was what he said, and at first she could only stare at him, dumbfounded. Then he added, 'All I mean is that I'm there if you need to talk. I'd like to know how you're coping, and if I can help in some way . . . What happened to Julia was dreadful; it can't be allowed to happen again, but it *could*, and no female will feel safe as long as the bastard who killed her is running free.'

'I suppose not.'

There was a nervous lull before he said, 'A thing like this makes everyone feel so helpless. The night Julia was here, I just couldn't take my eyes off her. I wanted to say something, but, well, bottled out. Then I saw her getting ready to leave, and I told myself, you're going to let her slip through your fingers, you can't just sit here, you've got to tell her what's on your mind or burst. If only I had, things might have been different. Who knows?'

'Exactly. No one knows.'

'Perhaps it would've changed things. Anyway, that's my story. I'm sorry if I kept you.'

'Don't mention it.' When Maggie started towards the door, he matched her step for step. Her cheeks were still tingling, yet she felt strangely flattered by his interest. When she turned to say goodbye, Dave Sessions was searching and patting his suit, drawing a slim black wallet from his inside breast pocket. 'This is totally impulsive of me, I know, but . . .' From the wallet he slid a card bearing his name and a business address in Roundhay. 'Call me if you feel you want to. If you don't, I'll understand.'

She would've laughed if she hadn't been so disorientated. He was practically asking her out. But she took the card anyway, looked at it once, then slipped it into the pocket of her coat. She would usually never have been so bold, but tonight she was Julia, and Julia was a freewheeling spirit. Julia would have seized every opportunity life sent her. And so she thanked him, turned, stepped through the doorway.

'Your name,' Dave Sessions called after her. 'I didn't get your name.'

Julia, she very nearly replied. She hesitated just long enough to be certain.

'Maggie.'

She smiled and peered up the arcade to see Christine running breathlessly towards her. Some distance beyond Christine, on Briggate, the others waited in a gossiping group where the van and the BMW were parked.

Christine's face was a picture of twinkling, lecherous mirth. 'So?' she said, snaking an arm around Maggie's. 'So? *So?*'

'So what?'

'You know what, you harlot! Hurry up, they're waiting. What happened with that debonair dreamboy? Out with it now. The whole dirt and nothing but the dirt. You may as well tell me or I'll be prising the truth out of you all night long.'

'It wasn't what you think.'

'Don't make assumptions about what I think. Out with it.'

Maggie glanced back as Christine led her away, but Dave Sessions had returned to his coffee.

'Did you give him your number?' Christine asked.

'No, but he gave me his.'

'My God, you must have the Midas touch. The man is a bronzed Adonis.'

'He's just a nervous, ordinary guy like any other,' Maggie laughed.

'Oh yeah. Sure. Ha ha.'

'Shut up. It was nothing.'

'Judging by that earthy tremor in your voice, I'd say it was more than nothing, wouldn't you? You'll call him of course, won't you?'

'I don't know. I can't think about it now. We're in the middle of a film shoot, Christine.'

'So we are.' Christine waited until they'd reached the top of the arcade before saying, 'Just a cautionary note, Mags. Did he approach you because you're dolled up like Julia? Is it you he's interested in or her? He probably wouldn't even recognize you without the make-up.'

Maggie shrugged, said nothing, though Christine had hit a nerve: she couldn't rule out the possibility. Pocketing her hands against the cold, she felt his business card slip between her fingers. 'It was just a silly moment,' she said at last. 'I wouldn't read too much into it if I were you.'

'If you say so.'

Five minutes later they were together in the back of the BMW, watching the film crew unloading their equipment outside V. It was too early to film inside the club. The place would be empty for at least another hour, and was unlikely to be crowded with dancers until midnight. Since it would be easier – far less of an organizational headache – to wait for the customers to arrive in their own time than to seek out two hundred extras for the indoor scenes, they would shoot the exteriors first.

'No one saw Julia arrive,' the director explained to Maggie, leaning in at Penhaligon's window. 'But a handful of punters noticed her inside, and a few saw her leave. The first shot we want is a breeze; you're stepping out of the night-club and being collected outside.'

'The driver who picked Julia up,' Linda said. 'Did anyone identify him?'

'Too dark,' Penhaligon said. 'We've had better luck with the car itself. We didn't get the registration number, but a van driver who was parked across the street saw a white Ford Fiesta kerb-crawling outside the club after midnight. That's the vehicle she got into. Two other witnesses corroborated the van driver's story.'

As he finished speaking, a pall of headlights flooded through the BMW from the rear, sending weird shadows scuttling across the detective's face like spiders. When the light faded, Maggie twisted to look through the rear window. A white Fiesta had parked two car lengths behind.

'So you know what you're doing?' Penhaligon said to Maggie.

'I think so. I come out of the foyer, stand on the pavement until the car pulls up. Then I hop inside. No problem. Did Julia talk to the driver *before* getting in?'

'According to our van driver, no. She simply leaned towards the car and opened the door. Which suggests that she knew the driver.'

'A white Fiesta,' Maggie murmured, half to herself.

'Does it mean something to you?' Penhaligon asked.

'No. Not really. Not yet anyway. I was thinking aloud.'

But that wasn't the whole truth, and she hoped he couldn't read the slight hesitant note in her voice. She'd remembered the summer again, the first weeks of the summer which she and Ian had spent together: an upbeat, sunkissed time which still gave her goose-bumps when she thought of it, for there had been no dark clouds on the horizon then – no Alison, no Julia Broderick.

They'd studied at each other's houses, sunbathed on Ian's patio while an aircraft marked a slow white snail's trail across the sky. They'd played tennis and sipped ice-cold beer in the park; fallen asleep in each other's arms in the shade of a tree overlooking the park's miles of green golf-course. In the evenings, Ian had driven her into Leeds, once to see The Orb play the university, once to L'America at the Corn Exchange, a night of high-spirited, high-perspiration dancing which had cost a fortune, lasted until three or four in the morning for those who could take it, and which she'd remember for a long time to come.

She remembered Ian's madcap driving too, but at least she'd *survived* to remember. It was as though another, demonic Ian took over once he slid in behind the wheel. In the end she'd had to plead with him to slow down while she covered her eyes with both hands. It wasn't the memory of his driving that bothered her now so much as the fact that his dad's car, the car he'd borrowed each time they went out and which he'd nearly run off the road several times, was a white Ford Fiesta.

But there were millions of identical vehicles on the road. Of course there were. It was an easy, convenient connection to make, but Ian *wasn't like that*. A thoroughgoing bastard, maybe; but never a murderer, never, no way. She knew him. She couldn't have fallen asleep in his arms on the grass in July without knowing him. The very idea of Ian kerb-crawling outside V after midnight seemed ridiculous, and in any case he hadn't known Julia Broderick, had he?

Well, *had* he?

Sometimes, Maggie, sometimes people can appear to be what they're not.

Her father's words returned to her again as the director signalled ready and she started from the car. No, people weren't always what they appeared to be. One way or another, Julia had found that out for herself. But never from Ian. Never.

12

It was almost eleven-thirty before the joint started jumping. From her table above the dance floor Maggie watched a peroxide blonde girl in the slightest white dress she had ever seen strutting across the floor, turning every head in the house. Under the strobing lights she looked like a spectre enveloped in smoke. Her arms and long, tan legs were a blur, her eyes were shut tightly. She was lost in music.

Maggie closed her eyes too in an effort to clear her thoughts. Something by New Order was hammering from the PA with enough force to worry her fillings. When she looked towards the director again, he was making a finger and thumb circle at her and mouthing something. The camera had stopped rolling at last. She'd been playing at being Julia, stepping in and out of cafés and cars, dancing herself blue in the face for so long now she'd forgotten what night this was. These few hours felt to her like a tough week's work. Christine and Linda had trudged home an hour earlier, and now she too felt ready to drop. At least the police had taken her for dinner to Da Mario's while they waited for V to warm up.

Seated across the table from Maggie was a young man wearing all black: jacket, polo shirt, jeans. His name was Gordon Howatt – another hunk, but in those clothes he might have been a funeral director. In fact he was a student from Linda's course, had met Julia twice, and fitted a description the police had of the man she'd been seen with at V. Or one of the men. According to Penhaligon, Julia had flirted with two or three others at the night-club. Like the peroxide blonde in the skimpy white dress, she'd moved across the dance floor, cutting in on whoever took her fancy, and had danced with them, no strings attached.

But one of the men might have left with her. Penhaligon's theory was that someone Julia hooked up with here had left V a few minutes before her to pick up his car. He'd arranged to meet Julia in front of the club, which was why she'd climbed in without trading small-talk first. She'd *expected* to be collected there, but by whom?

In any case, the car wasn't everything. The driver wasn't necessarily the killer. It was too soon to draw conclusions on that score, because nothing in this case was open and shut. With luck, the reconstruction would spark someone in the TV audience into action. It was scheduled for transmission next week. The best-case scenario was that someone out there knew the man that Julia left with, and would see the broadcast and phone. Worst-case scenario: while the reconstruction was showing, the same vital viewer would be tuned to another channel.

'I'm curious about something we *haven't* filmed,' Maggie said, leaning forward from the back seat while Penhaligon drove her home. 'All the reports keep mentioning the marks someone made on Julia's forehead. Two words. Why hasn't that been made public yet?'

'In the interests of the case,' Penhaligon said. 'It's routine procedure to withhold a few key details. You wouldn't believe the number of crank calls we get from people claiming responsibility for serious crimes. But they're easily eliminated as suspects if there are things about the case they *don't* know.'

'Has anyone claimed responsibility for Julia yet?'

'A couple, I believe. Sad, crazy people craving attention. Everything they knew they got from the media. There are so many of them out there.'

Maggie shivered. 'So I suppose it's too much to expect you to tell *me* what the words said.'

She couldn't see his face in the dark but he sounded to be smiling as he said, 'Yes, it is.'

'Jeez, and I don't even get *paid* for tonight's hard labour. Is there no reward in this life?'

'Well, you *could* congratulate yourself on a job well done,' Penhaligon said. 'You've given it your all, and helped probably more than you know. There's your reward. You should feel pleased with yourself. And if your people at work give you hell when you're late tomorrow morning –'

'They won't. They're good people.'

'There are good people in the world too, yes there are. It isn't all cranks and crazies. I hope you're not getting the wrong impression.'

'No, I'm not.' But, she thought, *but* . . . that doesn't mean I'm not outnumbered by cranks and crazies, does it? Just lately they've been crawling out of the woodwork everywhere. She wondered whether Julia had ever felt the way she felt now, like a magnet, drawing something strange and potentially deadly towards herself.

Moments later they were drawing up to the streetlit kerb outside her flat. A curtain parted at a ground-floor window as the BMW stopped, and a band of amber light settled across the detective's eyes, like a robber's mask, when he turned from the wheel to shake Maggie's hand.

'We'll be in touch,' he told her.

'Fine. And *I'll* be in touch if I learn anything new.'

Penhaligon climbed out and opened the door for her. She scrambled from the car, waved at the darkness inside the BMW where the other detective sat, then turned up the drive.

'Good-night, Julia,' Penhaligon said to her back.

She turned. 'Good-night, *who*?'

His hand flashed to his mouth, muffling a nervous, embarrassed laugh. For a moment it was easy to forget who and what he was; he'd become just an ordinary man whose guard had dropped for a second. 'Excuse me. Good-night, Maggie.'

'That's better. Now I can sleep safe in the knowledge of who I am.'

But she seriously doubted she'd be able to. Something had changed in her tonight, she knew. It wasn't anything she could pinpoint so soon; just a feeling. Until now, her life had been ordinary and safe, while Julia's had been so dramatic, so hyper. But tonight she, Maggie Waverly, had become the centre of attention – people were looking at *her*, marvelling at *her* – but more than that, she'd moved closer to Julia than ever before. She was beginning to understand her now, to see what had driven her, to understand her tastes, her point of view.

87

Climbing the stairs to the flat, she took out Dave Sessions' business card and looked at it. Her fingers were trembling. Was he another crank or just a genuine, lonely guy? She repocketed the card and knuckled tiredness from her eyes. You're tapping into something, she thought. That's what's happening, isn't it? That's what changed in you tonight. There's a whole other world out there – a world you've never known, but a world Julia inhabited until her last night on earth. And if there's an answer to this riddle, if there's a way to find out what happened, that's where you'll find it; in that world of night.

At last she took a deep breath and became Maggie again, leaving Julia behind her, outside in the cold, at least for now. Then she fished out her key and let herself into the flat.

13

Christine was nowhere in sight when Maggie came in, but Linda was still in the lounge. Her eyes were muted and pink, her cheeks were patchy. She couldn't disguise the fact that she'd been crying, but she wasn't about to advertise it either. With a brightness that caught Maggie off guard she said, 'Hey! We were beginning to worry about you, Mags. Or at least I was. My better half's been asleep for an hour. How did the rest of it go?'

'If that's what acting's about,' Maggie said, not bothering to remove her jacket before flopping down, 'you can keep it. My feet feel like balloons on the verge of bursting.' She slipped off the flat-soled leather shoes she'd borrowed from Christine, black to match her dress, and spread herself out, full length, on the sofa.

'Coffee?' Linda asked.

'Not the way you make it. I'll be out of my brain for hours and I need to sleep. Why aren't *you* asleep?'

'Not tired, I suppose.'

'But you have classes this morning. You should rest.'

'I know.' Linda was gazing into space as if transfixed by the patient tick of the digital counter on the Sharp CD player. A song by k.d. lang played soft as a whisper. 'But my mind's working overtime. I can't seem to turn it off.'

'Perhaps if you talked about whatever's bothering you.'

'I already did, with Christine. It isn't fair to burden you too.'

'Let me be the judge of that.' Maggie was studying Linda with a mixture of puzzlement and fear. Nothing Linda could tell her now could be any more worrying than the jumbled thoughts in her head. 'None of us are alone, Linda. We're all supposed to be friends here, aren't we? We share everything.'

Linda smiled, but her face was strained, and fresh tears weren't far away. 'You're an ace, Maggie. I'm glad it was you and not someone else.'

'You're glad *what* was me?'

'Who took Julia's place. We could easily have landed someone less suitable.'

There was a silence for perhaps a full minute. k.d. lang's voice rose and fell, tearing at Maggie's heart, though she wasn't absorbing the words. 'So what happened?' she asked. 'What upset you?'

'It's hard to put into words. It was so strange, tonight, to see you being Julia, so to speak, because it made me think again about what happened between her and Marcus while I was in Oz, and how I never really forgave her, not in my heart. And now I just wish I could see her again, and tell her . . .'

'But you still forgave Marcus, despite what he did. It takes two to tango, Christine said.'

'Damn right, don't think I don't know it.' She broke off. 'Sometimes I wonder whether I might've been better off if we'd never met, but here we are. I suppose I'm stuck with that louse.'

'You love him?'

She nodded, half-smiling. 'Unfortunately, yes – and in spite of him being such a bastard at times. There's no sense in that, is there?'

'I'm not sure that sense comes into it.'

Then Linda said suddenly, 'Maggie, don't be angry with me, I wasn't lying to you and Christine, but when we were in that detective's car I only gave you half the story.'

'About what?' Maggie looked at her, bewildered.

'About being with Marcus the night Julia died. I *did* go to Marcus's, but he wasn't at home. I spent an hour or two with his flatmate, Richie, playing cards and drinking and listening to sounds.'

'You were protecting Marcus? Covering for him?'

'In a way. Probably.'

'So where was he? Did he ever tell you?'

Linda smiled without humour. 'You know, it's so strange. The only thing I remember clearly from being with Richie was this bottle of Evian water he had on the table. We were joking about how Evian spells naïve backwards, like you *have* to be naïve to pay two pounds for a tiny bottle of the stuff in some night-club. I suppose that stuck with me because, later, I thought to myself: how can *you* be so naïve? Julia sets out for the evening dressed to kill, Marcus is nowhere to be seen, Richie hasn't a clue where he is, even though he's gadding about in Richie's VW, and you can believe whatever you want to believe, but if you believe everything Marcus tells you, you're nuts.

'Maggie, I tried so hard to assume the best. I didn't *want* to believe it was Marcus she saw that night. The first time I asked him he made a kind of face –' Linda

91

wrinkled her nose to demonstrate. '– and shook his head and went, Naaaah; like who do you think I am? Would I lie to you? He told me he'd been drinking – not with Julia but alone, without any friends. She'd *asked* to see him, and made quite a scene about it, apparently. She was more attached to Marcus than he was to her, as things turned out. But Marcus refused, there was a lot he had to think over. Anyway, that's what happened. That's the whole story. It's something and nothing, but I thought you should know.'

'You believe what he told you?' Maggie asked.

'Sure. Wouldn't you?'

'After everything he put you through? I'm not sure.'

A defensive note had crept into Linda's voice. 'Believe me, it takes time to get close to Marcus, and most people never do make head or tail of him; but he's a good person at heart, really he is. If only you could see him with my eyes.' She gave a slight, breathy laugh. 'Christine thinks he's a typical male pig, you know. And you want to hear something really funny? So do I.'

'Me too.'

They both laughed.

'Of course, I shouldn't judge someone I don't really know,' Maggie said. 'But Marcus always seems so cool towards me. I don't mean uncivil, just distant.'

Linda moved from her armchair to the stereo as the k.d. lang album finished, and ejected the disc. 'I've noticed that too. But don't worry. He's wary about new people. He's a little uptight until you get to know him, is all. Then again, maybe it's because when he saw you . . .' She stopped herself there.

'Yes?' Maggie prompted.

'Oh, nothing.' Linda packed the CD back in its case and selected another. A chill breeze of techno wafted through the room from the speakers.

'You were about to say something,' Maggie said. 'What was it?'

'Just something that crossed my mind when you two first met. I noticed how Marcus hardly ever looked at you or spoke to you, and it struck me that maybe he was seeing Julia again, and it scared him somehow. I mean, after splitting with her during the summer, and then this terrible business ... He's hurting just as badly as anyone.'

'You've been very understanding,' Maggie said as Linda sat down again. 'And very forgiving. After what he and Julia did, I'm amazed you still care.'

'Of course I care. Julia was special. So is Marcus, in his own peculiar way. Anyway, they were never malicious to *me* – inconsiderate maybe; inconsiderate definitely. It was something they had to work out for themselves.'

'He doesn't deserve you,' Maggie said warmly. She would have reached for Linda's hand if she'd been any less exhausted.

'Does anybody deserve anybody?' Linda shrugged. 'At least I have a clear mind on one score.'

'What's that?'

'Marcus may be a pig, but he's a harmless pig all the same. He would never have hurt Julia, even if he *was* lying about not meeting her that night, which I know he wasn't. He loved her. It just isn't something he could do.'

At last Linda settled, closing her eyes while the music washed over her.

Fair enough, Maggie thought. If not Marcus, then who? One thing I do know: someone out there *was* capable of killing; and still is. Tread carefully, kiddo. Tread carefully.

14

There were times when Maggie wished librarianship *could* provide the easy life Christine had joked about: peace and quiet, the smell of old books, an environment where she could put her feet up. But there was rain in the air today, and it was if all the people filing through the doors had chosen the library for shelter. For nearly three hours she had no time to think, no time to breathe. Hurrying books through the service point, Maggie felt her mind spinning. The constant bleep of the computer sounded like her heart rate being monitored; the flickering fluorescent lights overhead reminded her of the strobes on V's dance floor.

'Are you sure you're all right?' Joyce Durham asked during mid-morning coffee break. 'You're as white as a sheet. I'd give you the afternoon off if we weren't so understaffed.'

'I'm fine,' Maggie answered, but in fact she was weary and drifting, straining to keep her eyes open. Worse, without Julia's make-up and clothing she felt profoundly vulnerable, even dumpy. She'd lain awake half the night, longing to hear Julia's voice in the wind at her window: just a word or two would have settled her, given her a sense of what to do next. But the only words in her head when she woke to the buzzing alarm were her own: Don't do it, she'd thought. Don't go back to that night world again. You might find what Julia found and there'll be no one to help you, no one to keep you safe.

At least Mrs Gardineer didn't enter the library glaring and moaning, though she still managed to ignore Maggie altogether, even as she checked out her books. She took them in silence, twitching her umbrella as she made for the exit.

Definitely cuckoo, Maggie thought.

The lunch-hour gave her the time she needed to take the air and clear her head. By one o'clock, the rain was a fine drizzle she was glad to feel on her face, hands and neck. Revived, she strolled to Granary Wharf, ate a swift snack at the health food café in the midst of the Bohemian shops under the dark arches, bought a small rug made in Nepal and two black-and-white prints for her wall from Paradyllic.

Maggie had her own keys for the library, and, returning early, let herself in. The first of the afternoon's customers arrived just as Kate Bradshaw was unlocking the door, ten minutes later. It was the train-spotter, returning his mound of criminal case histories. Maggie stopped what she was doing – filing borrowers' requests for books and CDs – to attend to him.

'You got through these pretty quickly,' she said lightly.

Patrick Carver smiled nervously and tugged at his shirt collar. In fact he looked less like a train-spotter today, for he was dressed in a newish denim jacket and less ragged jeans. When he blinked and rubbed at his eyes, she realized he must be wearing contacts in place of his glasses.

'I have to read quickly,' he said, staring past her right shoulder. 'There's a lot of work piling up lately.'

'I see. I forget which course you said you were on.'

'Psychology.'

'That's it. How's it going?'

He watched while she checked the return dates in each of the books. 'Pretty well. No: pretty depressing, actually, when you have to study this kind of thing.'

'I can imagine.' She closed the last book cover and looked at him. As she did, his gaze fell away and he seemed to flush. 'Is that all?' she asked.

'Ah, yes. I'd better find some more reading now.'

'Happy browsing.'

But he still seemed reluctant to leave her. Maggie stacked the books in a pile on the counter, giving herself something to do until he moved on. He'd hovered like this the last time, she remembered. It didn't unnerve her, but she wished he'd simply say whatever was on his mind. Then he did.

'I've been watching you,' he said, tweaking his collar again.

'Watching me?'

'Yes, when I come in the library, I can't help noticing you . . . you know, doing your thing, going about your business.'

Maggie smiled; at least tried to. 'Well, we all have work to do.'

'But it's you I always notice, not whatever it is you're doing. I always think you're so serene.'

'Thank you. It isn't the word *I* would've used.'

He smiled, still reddening. And in the silence that followed Maggie couldn't stop herself thinking: Uh oh, he fancies you. That's why he's dithering, that's why he's shed the old rags he was wearing last time, and started wearing the contacts. He didn't come because he'd finished those books but to pick you up. Get me out of this!

'You talk as if you have been watching me for ages,' she said. 'I've only been here a short while.'

'I know. But I – I've seen you in other places too. In town.'

'You should've said hello, then.'

'I wasn't sure you'd recognize me without my books.'

Maggie glanced at the door, willing more customers to come. This morning she could have done without them, but now she needed to be occupied, if only to save her from the train-spotter's unwanted attention. Don't ask me out, she thought wearily. Don't make things any more complicated than they already are.

But then Patrick Carver said something that took her aback completely. His eyes were on the heap of books on the counter as he spoke.

'Don't get me wrong, please. I haven't been spying. I've been watching out for you.'

'Watching out for me?'

'You have to be careful, you know.'

'I . . . what?'

'You have to take care of yourself. It would be terrible if the same thing happened to you.'

'The same thing? What're you talking about?' But part of her understood; the part that Julia had let loose in her knew damn well what he meant. But how could *he* know that *she* knew?

'I'm sorry,' he said. 'This isn't the time or the place. I shouldn't have brought it up here.'

'Well, now that you have I think you'd better explain yourself.'

'No, not here. Somewhere else maybe. When you have time.' He turned away sharply.

'Wait,' she called after him, a little too loudly. An elderly couple in the reading section tutted and peered up from their newspapers as she moved from the service point. Joyce, huddled over the microfiche screen, blinked and continued her work. 'Wait right there, just a minute.'

But he'd said as much as he wanted to and now he was hurrying through the library towards the main door, forgetting any books he might've wanted. He glanced back at her, saw her coming, almost jogging, but kept walking straight ahead. Her footfalls sounded inordinately loud on the wooden floor. A gust of cool air washed into her face as he shouldered open the door and stepped out. He didn't slow down until Maggie reached the door, and by then he was on the pavement, ten or twelve paces ahead of her.

'Excuse me,' she said, 'but you're —'

'I'm sorry. I shouldn't have said what I did. I wish I could take it back.'

'But you can't. You more or less said I was in danger, didn't you? Well, didn't you?'

'No, I never. What I meant —'

'You know something, don't you? What do you know?'

'I saw,' he said. 'I saw —'

The thunder of a nearby train on the bridge above the street drowned out whatever he said after that. By the time its sound faded, Patrick Carver had glanced left and right along the busy street, chosen his moment and crossed. He stumbled quickly away along Stone Street, head down, hands pocketed. Maggie stared after him until the cold threatened to layer her whole body with goose-bumps. Finally, trembling, she retreated indoors.

A freckled, bespectacled woman waited at the service point with a mound of paperback horse-riding novels. Distracted, Maggie ran the light pen quickly over their bar-codes, handing them over without comment.

'Whatever happened to service with a smile?' the woman clucked, turning away.

The first time she'd noticed the train-spotter he'd struck her as mildly eccentric; a little weird and withdrawn, if harmless enough. Now she saw him in a new, more unsettling light. He'd been trying to warn her about something; something that might be about to happen. But how could he know? Had he seen the future? Not necessarily, but he *had* seen something; he'd been on the point of telling her so when the train drowned out his voice.

Of course, Patrick Carver had been following Julia, or at least that was what Julia had believed. As Maggie put down the light pen she saw one of his books, *True Crimes: Profiles of Six Mass Murderers*, staring up at her from the counter. No, you don't get off so lightly, she thought. You've got a story to tell, Mr Train-spotter. You've opened a fresh can of worms here today, and you can't walk away from it now.

15

She would talk to Patrick Carver in her own time, but by seven o'clock when the library closed she wanted only to be at home. The phone was ringing when she entered the flat, but neither Christine nor Linda were there to answer it. Dropping the prints and the rug from Paradyllic on the sofa, she fumbled through the dark to pick it up.

'Hello?' she said. And again, when no one replied, 'Hello? Who's calling?'

It was the same as before. All she could hear was a breathless, static-charged silence. The caller without a voice had been waiting for her to come home before dialling, timing his call to meet her. Perhaps he'd watched while she entered the building; perhaps he was watching her now. In a panic, she swung away from the window, though in the darkness it was doubtful whether anyone could see her.

'I'm going to hang up now. Before I do, let me tell you what I think of you . . .'

'I only wanted to hear your voice,' someone said. It was spoken in a whisper, and at first she failed to recognize it. Gripping the phone tightly, she leaned against the wall, supporting herself in case her legs should give way.

'Are you there?' the voice said. 'Maggie, is that you?'

'Ian! Jesus! You gave me the fright of my life. I thought it was him again.'

'Who?'

'Never mind. Why didn't you speak when I answered?'

'I didn't know what to say. My mind went blank.'

'So what's new?'

'Very funny. Is everything all right? You sound flustered.'

'That's a mild way of putting it, but yes, I am. What do you want?'

'To apologize, if you'll let me. To tell you I'm sorry.'

'For what? For threatening me?' She was gripping the receiver so firmly now her nails were scouring her palm. 'Correct me if I'm wrong, but I think you said I'd be sorry: your exact words. Go ahead, Ian, if you want to apologize. See how far it gets you.'

'You're not making this any easier for me.'

'Pardon me. How easy do you want it?'

She pictured him gritting his teeth, forcing himself not to explode. 'I spoke out of turn the other day,' he said dimly. 'What came out of my mouth . . . wasn't what I intended.'

She still had a wild, impossible urge to reach down the phone and slap his face. 'Go on,' she said flatly, reaching through the dark for the nearest lamp. Switching it on, she carted the phone to an armchair and melted into it. 'You spoke out of turn. And?'

'God, you drive a hard bargain.'

'Me? I don't enjoy being walked over, that's all. I'll

say it again: you can't pick people up and put them down to suit yourself, Ian. They run out of patience eventually.'

His sigh produced a thin, reedy hiss in her ear. 'Fair enough. I know what you're saying. I was just hoping we might patch things up, but slowly, in your own time.'

'It'll have to be. My diary is bulging. I have so many admirers out there, you know.'

'Maggie, what's wrong with you? You've never been like this before.'

'Like what?'

'I can't say exactly. But you sound different somehow; so hyped up. This isn't just about you and me, is it?'

She faltered before answering. Yes, she was feeling hyped up, and the reason had little to do with Ian. She'd hardly spared him a thought since the weekend. '*Things* are different now, not just me,' she said quietly. 'I'm living a new kind of life these days, mixing with new people. That's what's changed.'

'Then I can't say I like what it's doing to you. You're much harder now. You sound as hard as nails, Mags.'

'All the better to resist you with, Ian.' She exhaled slowly, sinking a little further into the chair. 'But at least I've learned one thing since we were seeing each other. Sometimes we have to be hard to protect ourselves.'

'Fair enough. If that's how you're happy to be.'

'I'm OK. Really. I'm still the same old . . .' Julia, she almost said, but corrected herself just in time. 'I'm still the Maggie you always knew. And you're the same old Ian I always knew.'

There was a long, awkward pause before he spoke again. 'I still care about you, Mags.'

'I know. And I do about you, believe it or not.'

'We could still meet for coffee now and then, couldn't we?'

'I wouldn't rule it out.' She was relaxing now, regaining her composure. She didn't want to hurt him, not intentionally, but it was impossible to ignore what he'd done, how he'd made her feel when she saw him with Alison.

She'd first noticed them together upstairs in the St John's Centre, one Saturday afternoon in late August. They were standing hand in hand outside Jumbo Records when Maggie looked up from the CDs she was sifting through in the sale rack inside. She'd caught Ian's eye as she turned towards the till clutching her finds – the first Sugar album, the last Happy Mondays – and there was a moment, a small but significant moment as she started to look away when Ian kissed Alison squarely on the mouth, brushing his fingers lightly against her throat. As she reached the till, Maggie felt a sharpness twist in her gut like a knife. Slapping the CD boxes on the counter, she gazed at the assistant in speechless horror. Ian, she thought. How could you?

He'd kissed Alison intentionally, knowing she would see, and he'd done it to hurt her; it couldn't have been for any other reason, and in that instant she felt a hot flush of hatred that she hoped she'd never feel for anyone again.

But she didn't hate him now. She didn't even feel sorry for him, for that matter, even though pity was all he really wanted from her, now that he and Alison were history. Maggie had read a magazine article once that made more sense to her now than ever: in any relationship, the article said, there was always one partner who was *up* and one who was *down*. Well, Ian had kept her down for long enough, and now she was up. She'd changed, become stronger. She'd become more like Julia, and no one could take that away from her, not even Ian. She didn't need to hit out at him now. She wasn't angry any more. She'd moved on. Besides, he might even be able to help her.

'Let me ask you something,' she said, 'while I've got you captive on the phone. This might sound an odd question to you.'

'I'm easy. Go ahead.'

'Does your dad still drive that white Fiesta? The one you used to take me out in?'

'No, not the same one. He traded it in and bought a new model: gun-metal grey this time. Why do you ask?'

'Just wondering. I knew it couldn't have been you, Ian.'

'What couldn't?'

'Nothing. Thanks for setting my mind at ease.'

'Maggie, you're not making sense.'

'Maybe not. If you could see things from my side, you'd understand. But you can't. You're just an insensitive pig.'

'And I thought you said you still cared about me.'

'I do, but it doesn't make you any less of a pig.' She smiled at that, and the heaviness she'd felt since she answered the phone finally left her. 'Ian, why don't you call again in a week or two and maybe we'll have that coffee? Just don't hurry me, that's all. Things are likely to be hectic for a while. There's so much I still have to do.'

'Work, is it?'

'Kind of, yes.' That's right, she thought. I have to go to work; I have to do this for Julia's sake. 'Now isn't a good time to be seeing you, do you understand? Later maybe, but things will never be the same; I can tell you that now.'

'I see.' He sounded crestfallen, but at least when he rang off she didn't feel under threat from him. For once, she'd managed to confront him without lapsing into melodramatics – tears, accusations, bitterness.

Putting down the phone, she drew the curtains, then carried the rug and prints to her room. She spread the rug on the floor between the foot of the bed and the dresser, then stood at full stretch, hoisting the prints to the top of the wardrobe for safekeeping. She'd need to find a hammer and nails to hang them.

A cloud of dust stirred as she slid the prints back on top of the wardrobe. She couldn't leave them up there; they'd be ruined. There were dusters in the kitchen, though. Fetching two, she climbed on to a chair. Dust puffed into her face, prickling her skin, as she began cleaning. She'd given the room a quick going over after moving in, but had neglected the wardrobe top until now. By the looks of it, so had every tenant before her; this was beyond filthy: it was truly disgusting. The dust had formed a thick layer. She steadied herself against the wardrobe as she sneezed, violently enough to rock the chair underneath her.

As her vision cleared, Maggie noticed a squat, dark object jammed way back, between the wardrobe and the wall. It had almost slipped down out of sight, and would still do so if she didn't take care in retrieving it. Her heart gave a quick, nervous leap as she clawed it towards her. How many tenants passed through rooms like this every year, leaving their possessions behind – small, trivial things they mightn't miss later? Perhaps what she was handling now had belonged to Julia. It was a black, multipocketed shoulder bag.

Dust fluttered about her as she lowered it to the floor. Her face was itching unbearably, she wanted to sneeze again, but the bag wasn't nearly as filthy as the top of the wardrobe she'd taken it from. It had the look and feel of real leather.

Maggie unzipped one of the pockets at random. Here was a provisional driver's licence and a two-year-old student Railcard with a passport-sized colour photograph of a girl Maggie recognized at once as Julia.

She stared at it for a moment, heart racing. In the photo, Julia was smiling so easily, it was impossible to imagine anyone hating or wanting to hurt her. Her corn-coloured hair was cropped shorter than on the police poster, and she was wearing lipstick, red as blood. It was a shade or two deeper than the kind Maggie had worn last night, but it didn't overpower Julia's face; even in this tiny photo-booth shot, she seemed to glow, Maggie thought. There was a radiance about her, in the light of her eyes, as though she knew something that no one else did.

'You really were something special,' Maggie told the photograph. 'Jeez, if only I'd known you. We would've been so close, I know we would. Just like sisters.'

Ian would never have dumped Julia for Alison, that was for sure. He would never have treated *her* so unthinkingly. He wouldn't have dared. Keeping the

Railcard, Maggie returned the driver's licence to the zipper-pocket and tried another, then another. The rest of the bag was empty, apart from a small, blue address book and an eyebrow pencil. Moving to the dresser, she put the pencil in her own make-up bag and sat for a time, scanning pages of the address book.

It was unused, save for some names and telephone numbers Julia had scribbled across the first few pages. She hadn't bothered to list them alphabetically. Mum and dad were here; so was Hayden; then came several entries which meant nothing to Maggie – Ros, Peter K., Angie, Paul Hoffman. All of these carried the same area code as her parents' and Hayden's numbers. They dated from a time before Julia moved to Leeds, Maggie decided. Old friends, most likely.

Now she picked up the student Railcard again, laying it on the dresser top, then taking out the eyebrow pencil and a lipstick from her make-up kit. As she added a line of colour here, a hint of shade there, she checked her reflection in the mirror against Julia's photograph. She pursed her lips and a shudder ran through her. The resemblance was striking.

'I'm going to help you, Julia,' she whispered. 'I'm going to find out what happened to you. But you'll have to show me how.'

Then she took the black dress from the wardrobe and laid it out on the bed before undressing. She'd left work weary and drowsy tonight, but this unexpected find had inspired her. So much for slobbing out and retiring early to bed. It was time to become Julia again.

16

'What *are* you doing?' Christine's exclamation stopped Maggie in her tracks as she left her room, dressed to kill and ready to dance. 'You're not going out like that again, surely not.'

'Maggie?' Linda said. The girls had arrived home from college together; the door to the flat was still ajar. Linda gave it a firm push and it closed with a thump that made Maggie flinch. 'The police reconstruction is over and done with, remember?'

'I know. I know all about it.' Maggie stood facing them across the lounge, half-embarrassed, unable to meet their eyes. She felt her cheeks burn as the others exchanged a glance. 'But this is for *me*. I need to go over it again. If I could just –'

'You're crazy.' Christine's tone was hard and cool as metal. 'Are you looking for trouble, or what?'

'We all need to know what happened to Julia.'

'And supposing you find out the hard way? Supposing you wind up like her? What will *that* achieve?'

Maggie shrugged. 'I'll be on my guard. I won't make the same mistake she made.'

'Can you be sure?' Christine stepped forward, taking her arm. 'Julia was streetwise, and look what happened to her. She wouldn't have walked into trouble with her eyes wide open. One thing we *do* know is that whoever killed her suckered her first. She wouldn't have put herself in a tricky situation with someone she didn't know or didn't trust.'

'Nor will I.'

'We've lost one Julia already,' Linda pleaded. 'Don't put us through it all over again, Mags.'

Maggie looked at her, saying nothing.

'You want my opinion?' Christine volunteered. 'You're turning into Sister Hyde or something. Just look at you. This *isn't* you, Mags.'

'I'm aware of that. Do you think I don't know what I'm doing?'

'I'm sure you don't. You're playing with fire, is what. The killer is still out there, remember. This isn't a game.'

Maggie squirmed away from Christine's grasp as if it were meant to constrain or hurt her. 'I know you're both doing this for my sake,' she said. 'I know you have my best interests at heart, but –'

'You never even knew her,' Linda protested.

'But I'm getting to know her. As well as you ever did. I'm living in her room, aren't I?'

'So what?' Christine's hands were on her hips. 'So *what*?'

'And we look alike. You said so yourself.'

'I never said alike; I probably said similar. But it's only a passing resemblance, and only then when the light hits you a certain way or when you're wearing that face-paint.'

'It's more than that, and you know it.'

They stared at her in bewilderment. After a moment Linda said, 'You've really made your mind up about this, haven't you? And there's nothing anyone can say to change it.'

Maggie gave a curt nod but kept her lips sealed. The tip of her tongue tasted lipstick: floral, like Beaujolais.

'Then we ought to go with her,' Christine told Linda. 'It's the least we can do. Someone ought to be there to watch over her.'

'That's exactly what I don't want,' Maggie said calmly. 'Don't worry, because I won't be taking any stupid risks. All I plan to do is put myself in her shoes for a while, try to see through her eyes; talk to a few people, the kind of people she might have met. I don't plan to go home with anyone.'

'Nuts,' Christine said, tapping her temple with a forefinger. 'You've lost your marbles. If you think what you're doing is helping, think again. You can't guarantee *anything* once you're out there.'

'It's hard enough on us all without having to see you like this,' Linda said as the telephone rang. 'Please, Mags . . .' She brushed past Maggie on her way to answer it.

'You should let us come too,' Christine insisted as Linda snared the receiver. 'We wouldn't be interfering; just keeping an eye on you from a distance.'

'No. That isn't the way I want it.'

'Why not?'

'As long as you and Linda are there, I'll be with you somehow and not out on my own, the way Julia was. You didn't watch over *her* that night, did you?'

'No, but if we'd known what was on the cards, we would have been there like a shot. Or we would've stopped her from going. We would've tried talking her out of it. See sense, Mags, for God's sake. This really isn't a good idea.'

'Damn right,' Linda said, overhearing. Then she told the receiver, 'No, I was talking to Maggie.' There was a silence while the caller spoke. Then she said, 'Sure, but later. I'll call you back. Right. See you later. That was Marcus,' she said, hanging up. 'If he could see you now, Mags, he'd flip; I swear.'

'I've got to go,' Maggie said after a lull. 'I won't be too long.'

'You'd still better call us from time to time,' Christine suggested, 'if only to let us know where you are. We'd both feel a lot easier if you would.'

'OK. That's no trouble.'

'And you'd *better*,' Linda said, waggling a finger. 'Because if we haven't heard from you by nine, we'll be calling the cops.'

'I'll be in touch,' Maggie said. 'Don't worry.'

'That's asking too much. We're going to worry,' Christine said. 'We ought to hate you for doing this to us, Mags. Just be careful.'

'Careful is my middle name,' Maggie said, smiling, she hoped, reassuringly.

Or at least it had been until now, she thought.

Adjusting her bag on her shoulder – the bag which had been Julia's, and which she'd now wiped clean and claimed for herself – she dodged past Christine, unbolted the door and stepped out without looking back.

17

Her first port of call was Little Rico's coffee bar, where a handful of customers she recognized from last night lounged on the stools, blowing the steam from their cups. They stared and muttered among themselves as Maggie crossed to the counter, found somewhere to sit and called for an espresso.

A man on her immediate right – in his late twenties, with thinning, receding hair – turned towards her. 'You were in here last night, weren't you?'

'Me and a few others, yes.'

'The TV crew; that's right.' He snapped his fingers as the memory fell into place. 'Of course, I should've realized who you were straight away. What was all that about, then?'

'It was a police reconstruction. They'll broadcast it early next week.'

'So you're going to be a TV star, are you?'

'Not likely. But if it helps the police, I'll be happy.'

'Who were you supposed to be in this film, then?' He was staring at her hands, as if checking for rings. His lazy eyes blinked slow as an owl's. 'Or is that something you can't discuss?'

'Her name was Julia Broderick.' Maggie met his

gaze and, briefly, he seemed to retreat into himself. 'She's been in all of the papers.'

'I know. I've heard the story. Who hasn't? I saw her picture on a poster somewhere; and if you don't mind my saying, she was a very pretty girl, very pretty.'

'Why should I mind you saying so?'

'Well, I meant that so are you. She didn't wear as much make-up, though. Not on the poster.'

'Did you ever see her in this place before?' Maggie asked.

'No, but then I don't come in here regularly. Last night I had to work late. Tonight I missed my train and found myself with an hour to kill. So here I am again.' Picking up his spoon, he clinked it noisily in the half-empty cup before him, then set it down again. 'Yes, it's a crying shame. Such a pretty girl. Such a waste.'

OK, Maggie thought. The man doesn't know anything, but not everyone you meet is likely to. Swivelling slightly on her stool, she cast a glance over the rest of the bar. There was no sign of Dave Sessions, the hunk in the suit. She still had his card, but there was no point in calling his office now, after business hours. In any case, it made more sense to arrange a rendezvous during daylight, perhaps one lunch-time.

Now she focused on the furthest corner of the bar, where a young couple wearing cowboy boots and broad-brimmed black felt hats were sitting. Both were smoking cigarettes. The girl, whose long blonde hair tumbled about her shoulders, glanced twice at Maggie before giving her partner a nudge.

Everyone's watching, Maggie thought with a shudder. But that's the whole point, that's why you're here, isn't it? Just keep your cool; remember, they're seeing *her*, not you.

She turned back to her coffee as 'The Drowners' by Suede began playing at low volume behind the flourishing plants. *You're taking me ohh-vah*, the chorus droned, and Maggie thought: Is that appropriate or what?

Then she jumped, because someone – not the balding man at her side – had just laid a hand on her shoulder. She turned to find the blonde girl hovering over her, cigarette still held at the tilt in her right hand. The smoke crept upwards in a fluttering, fine blue line.

'This is so uncanny,' she said before Maggie could speak. 'I was just saying to Scott, you must be some relation, am I right?'

'Whose relation?' Maggie said, as if she needed to ask.

'Julia's. Julia Broderick's. You know who I'm talking about?'

'Yes, of course. But I never –'

'I'm sorry. My mistake.' The girl held up a hand by way of apology. 'Seeing you come in here just now was like seeing a ghost. A visitation, y'know? This is really so weird. I'm – I'm sorry to have bothered you.'

'Wait,' Maggie said before the girl could retreat any further. 'If you knew Julia I'd be grateful if you could tell me about her. Anything would help.'

'Why? Are you from the police?'

'Do I look like I'm from the police? I'm just curious. Some of my friends knew her well.'

'They must be devastated.' Switching the cigarette to her left hand, she offered her right, and Maggie gave it a half-hearted shake. 'The name's Sally Gregson. I knew her from university, but not well. We were in the same sociology class, hung around together during the first term, but sort of drifted apart later on.'

'I see.'

'You could've been sisters, really you could.'

Maggie smiled faintly.

Sally took a quick hit on her cigarette. 'It scares me to think of the psychos out there, the people who'd do this kind of thing. She might've got up a few people's noses in her time, but she really didn't deserve *that*.'

Maggie shifted on her seat. She felt a sudden rush of nervous adrenalin, as if she were about to hear something startling, something more than mere speculation. 'The way I heard it, Julia was always well liked by everyone. I never heard a bad word against her.'

'Then you've been listening to the wrong people.' Sally reached past Maggie, drawing an ashtray across the counter, crushing out her cigarette in it. She glanced briefly towards the corner where she'd been sitting, then leaned closer, lowering her voice, the brim of her hat brushing Maggie's brow. '*We* could've been friends, if she hadn't been so . . .'

'Yes?'

'Do you mind if I sit for a minute?'

'Be my guest.'

'She had this incredible need to be noticed,' Sally said, easing on to a stool at Maggie's left. 'She was unbelievably demanding. For instance, whenever we took coffee breaks or went out together during that first term, it was always *her* we ended up discussing. Like, her problems were the only ones that concerned her; they were the centre of her world. She really wasn't interested in anything *I* had to say. In fact, I never met anyone so preoccupied with themselves. If you ask me, she was very insecure.'

'Is that why you stopped seeing her? Because you thought she was selfish?'

'Not exactly. Only partly. It was the *way* she sought attention that bothered me.' Again, she glanced back at her partner, who was watching, his face set and quizzical. 'My boyfriend, Scott over there, was the reason. Julia did everything she could to take him away from me, I swear.'

Maggie regarded her blankly. This didn't sound like Julia at all. 'Go on,' she said.

'Nothing actually happened; we might as well get that straight, for a start. But during lunch break, y'know, Scott would wait for me at a table in the refectory, always the same wobbly table for two; four at a push. Usually his class finished ten or fifteen minutes before mine. Once or twice Julia ducked out of sociology early. I can't remember the excuses she gave, but when I got to the refectory I found her sitting there with Scott. Well, more than just sitting with him; draping herself over him, is nearer the truth.'

'And Scott?'

'He was attracted; you could see that plainly enough. But he never encouraged her, not the way some would've done. Quite the opposite. In fact Scott once told me Julia was chasing him *because* he'd resisted her. I know this sounds dreadful, but maybe he became a kind of challenge to her, because she really could've had any guy she wanted. She was the kind that they look at twice when she walks in the room, you know? At *least* twice.'

'Did you ever confront her about this?'

'We fell out in the end; she claimed she hadn't done anything wrong, and didn't want trouble, but I didn't swallow *that* for one minute. Besides, there were phone calls too. She kept calling the flat where Scott was living with these two art students, old friends of his . . . all times of night. Once, when I was there, I answered the phone and she hung up on me. She didn't actually speak but she didn't have to; I *knew* it was her. You can sense these things. She made life pretty tough for us for a while. She wasn't the angel I keep hearing people saying she was.'

Maggie sipped her espresso, her gaze shifting slowly from Sally to Scott, in the corner. No, she thought; this is really too much. Sally must be thinking of someone else, because Julia would never have behaved like that, and certainly not over Scott. The young man in the corner was handsome in his way, if scruffily unshaven, but there was nothing about him that would've driven Julia to distraction; she was too smart, too strong, too loyal. For one thing she had Hayden, and pursuing other men for the sake of her ego simply wasn't her style. She was better than that.

Besides which, there was Marcus. Fair enough, she *had* lapsed there, but Julia had broken off with *him*, not the other way around, and she'd done so in part to spare Linda's feelings, in part out of loyalty for Hayden. No, whatever took place between Julia and Scott had been a flash in the pan, and Sally had over-reacted.

'Still,' Sally was saying now, 'forgive and forget, right? We can't hold grudges for ever.'

'Of course not. And you and Scott are still together. She didn't cause you so much damage after all.'

'I guess she didn't.' Sally was staring dreamily into space as she added, 'But if that was how she conducted herself among friends, just imagine –'

'You were never Julia's friend,' Maggie said abruptly, defensively, with such hostility she startled even herself. Sally's eyes widened. 'Friends wouldn't smear a girl's memory the way you did just now. You were jealous of her, is all. Whatever happened was your problem at least as much as hers.'

At first, Sally seemed at a loss for words. Her lips parted, but no sound emerged. 'Excuse *me*,' she said finally. 'I was trying to be sociable. I didn't mean to upset you.'

'I'm not upset. I'm just defending someone who can't be here to defend herself.' But there was anger in her voice, and a tightness in her throat that felt like tears.

'Let me tell you something,' Sally said, getting up. The balding young man was rattling his spoon again, as if to stop himself overhearing. 'When I first came over here, you struck me as being really approachable, really open, and I wanted to help. But there's another side to you. Just like there was another side to her. And believe me, Julia wasn't an angel. Ask your friends, why don't you? Ask them what she was *really* like.'

'I already have,' Maggie told Sally's back as she turned away, flustered. 'They loved her in spite of herself.'

18

There were several watering holes between Rico's and V that might have attracted Julia. The nearest was Harvey's, on Merrion Street, a trendy café-bar bustling with Bohemian students most nights of the week. The minute Maggie came through the door, into the smoke and the laughter, she had to resist an urge to turn and walk straight out again. Four young men seated by the large front window gawked with mindless, glazed eyes as she crossed to the counter and ordered a white wine. At tables far and near, conversation dwindled to a mutter.

Of course, these students would be well aware of Julia. Some might even have been in her class. 'Who does she think she is?' someone whispered as Maggie took a seat at a spare table. Others continued to stare, puzzled and disapproving. Did they resent her because she resembled Julia, or was Julia the object of their anger?

What *were* you really like? she wondered, wishing Julia could answer. Are you hiding something from me? Something about yourself you wouldn't like others to know?

She took one brief sip of wine, then scraped back her chair, ready to leave. No one was likely to come forward here; there was no point in staying. She hadn't quite risen to her feet, however, when a hand settled over her shoulder, pressing her down again.

At first, when she saw the man smiling down at her, she couldn't put a name to the face. Then he said, 'Dave Sessions, remember? Of course you do. Do you mind?'

Before Maggie could answer, he'd seated himself opposite her, still smiling. He was much as she remembered him, in a spotless suit, except that he'd stripped off his tie and unfastened the top button of his shirt. He was drinking a Margarita with salt round the rim of the glass. 'I thought you'd seen me when you came in,' he explained. 'I waved, but you didn't react. Are you waiting for someone?'

'Not exactly.'

'Good, then I'm not intruding. Drink?'

She lifted her wine glass two inches from the table, set it down again. 'Thanks; no thanks.'

'Hope I wasn't being too forward, before, when we spoke. That is, I hope you didn't get the wrong impression.'

Maggie shrugged. 'Well, I still have your card. I haven't thrown it away yet.'

'At least that's a start, then. I imagined you would.'

'But I'm not sure I would've called you for a while, or ever.'

Dave Sessions nodded, as if he understood why. The muscles of his face had tightened. 'You probably thought I was some crank trying to pick you up, am I right?'

'It did cross my mind. I couldn't be sure whether you were interested in me, or in Julia.'

'Both actually. Do you mind if I ask you a question?'

'Depends on the question.'

'Why are you doing this?' He was leaning across the table, the fingers of both hands laced together in front of him. 'Why are you still playing the part? The reconstruction is over now, isn't it?'

'Maybe this makes me feel good,' she said, fingering her glass. 'Or maybe I dress this way all the time. How would you know?'

'Come on. Unless you're one mixed-up kid, this just isn't you; I think I can tell *that* much about you. You're looking for something, aren't you? You're not doing this for kicks.'

'I want the truth, just like everyone else. This is my way of trying to find it. I figured that if I could walk in her shoes for a while –'

'I assume your friends have already told you you're crazy.'

'They have.'

'And nothing they or anyone else says will stop you.'

She nodded. 'Anyway, what does this matter to you? You were just a witness; someone who saw Julia walk in and out of a coffee bar. If you'd *known* her, if you'd been a close friend of hers –'

'Supposing I *had* known her? Supposing I had?'

A slow, cold, sinking sensation settled over her then; she held Dave Sessions' gaze until the need to look away overpowered her. His expression was one of confidence, of knowing. He wasn't just supposing. 'Then you've been lying to the police,' she said firmly. 'And you've also been lying to me. You saw her and wanted to talk to her but bottled out: that's what you said.'

'I didn't tell the police the whole story. Why? Because, like you, I wanted to know more. I thought there might be something I could do. And besides . . .' He trailed off, seeming to need to weigh his words carefully before going on. 'Besides, if I'd told the police the whole truth, things wouldn't have looked too good for me. I might've come under suspicion.'

'Why?' She tried to keep her voice low, to a whisper, but it came out harshly, a hiss that drew stares from adjacent tables. 'On second thoughts, don't answer that. Tell *them*, tell the cops. You can't give one version of your story to them and another to me. Jesus, what am I doing, sitting here listening to you?'

Perhaps this was exactly what she'd been looking for. Perhaps here, at last, was someone who could tell her what she wanted to know. Even so, she needed suddenly to be free of him; to put a safe distance between herself and Dave Sessions before this went any further. If he was capable of lying, what else was he capable of?

She took to her feet very slowly, almost reluctantly, but Merrion Street looked dark and deserted, and she didn't want to flee only to have him follow, to corner her in some still dark alley where no one would see.

'Please wait,' he said.

'Everyone's watching. You can't do anything as long as we're here.'

He stared at her open-mouthed. 'You think I . . . Jesus God, you couldn't be more wrong. I never . . . I would never . . . Sit down, you bloody fool, and listen.'

Maggie glanced cautiously around the bar. Most of the clientele had drifted back into conversation, and the route to the door was clear. She perched on the edge of her wicker chair, ready to sprint at the first sign of trouble. 'Run it by me again,' she said. 'Tell me what you know or I'll be on the phone to the police so fast you won't have time to finish your drink. How did you get to know her?'

Suddenly, for the first time, he looked self-conscious and small, so small he seemed to be visibly shrinking inside his suit. 'I didn't exactly know her, not as friend, but we did spend time together that night, after Rico's.'

'You left there together?'

'No, what I told you before about that was true. I regretted not having the nerve to approach her there and then. So I sat there, helpless, watching her go, and I said to myself: There, you blew it! You'll never see her again, and what did you have to lose?

'I paid my bill in a hurry and ran into the pedestrian precinct. There was no sign of Julia there, of course. I was too late. I'd parked close by, but when I got to the car I just kept walking, further up Briggate, cursing myself. I knew it was only a passing thing; I wasn't going to spend the rest of my life looking for her, but she *was* the kind of girl that knocks a man sideways, fills him with, well, with fear. Then I turned down a side-street, looking for a pub, when I saw her again. I just couldn't believe my luck.'

'So you followed her?'

Dave Sessions stared into his drink. 'But not very far. There was a moment on Kirkgate when I completely lost her – a crowd of punters came out of the cinema – but when I'd pushed past them I saw her talking to this boy further along the street. Arguing more than talking, I thought. There was traffic, and I couldn't hear anything much at all, but Julia was throwing her arms about and the kid looked upset – upset or angry, and trying to grab hold of her arm. She sort of pulled away from him then, and said something, and then he backed away, like she'd slapped him. She *hadn't* slapped him, but there was a look in her eye as if she could have done much worse. Then she ran inside V and didn't come out again. She looked pretty shaken when she went in.'

'I see.' Maggie's head was spinning, her thoughts convoluted as cobwebs. 'The boy she was arguing with . . . had you ever seen him before?'

'No, and I doubt I'd recognize him again. He had his back to me – I would've guessed about five-five, five-six tall, no more – but the light from V was on Julia's face. Lit her up as if she were on stage. The kid sort of slunk away after she'd gone. He didn't follow her inside, but I did.' He paused. 'You haven't touched your drink. Shall I get you something else now?'

'No. Please go on.' She doubted she'd be able to swallow it anyway.

'We met on the dance floor,' Dave Sessions said. 'To begin with, at least, we were fooling, dancing together. It was too loud to talk, but we spent a long time just looking, taking each other in. Dancing and looking and grinning. She seemed to be coming round from whatever upset her before, and by the time we'd taken a table together and bought drinks, she was laughing, flirting. I don't think she ever told me her name; I never got around to telling her mine. It was more than I'd hoped for. She wasn't there to meet anyone. She seemed very freewheeling. Then, after a couple of drinks, she started to change.'

'Change? In what way?'

'Hard to say. She became distracted; started asking where the telephone was. She disappeared for a while, I suppose to make a call, and when she came back it was, well, as if she was looking for someone else. She sat there, touching my hand on the table, but scanning all the faces in the place, hardly even aware of me . . .

'So, I said, Look, if you're waiting for someone . . . But Julia shook her head: No, no, I'm sorry, I'll explain later on, she said. I asked if she wanted to leave but she didn't reply. I'd lost her completely. She'd switched herself off, just like that.' He snapped his fingers. 'So I said that *I* was ready for home, and in case she wanted a lift, I'd bring the car round the front and she could meet me there, but I wouldn't wait. She didn't leave with me then, and I didn't expect to see her outside, but there she was, about ten minutes later.'

'You were driving a white Fiesta,' Maggie said dreamily. She could see the scene clearly now; could see herself squeezing into the passenger seat, just as Julia had, while the camera rolled.

'How did you know?' Dave Sessions asked, frowning.

'It doesn't matter. It isn't important. What happened after that?'

He took a long, studious swallow from his glass. 'What happened was just plain weird. I mean, Julia wasn't your typical girl; anything but. She wanted me to drive her home, to her flat. Fair enough, it was on my way. And she started to relax as we drove. She covered my hand with hers on the steering wheel, and in a very weary little girl's voice invited me inside for coffee when we got there.'

Julia, how *could* you? Maggie thought, briefly covering her eyes with her fingertips. You only just met the man, for Chrissakes!

'This is so hard to take,' she said.

'How so?'

'You're talking about someone else, not the Julia I've come to know. She *wasn't* like that.'

'Did anyone ever *really* know her?' he wondered.

Maggie gave a shrug. Evidently not. 'Did you go with her?'

'I might as well be honest. I wasn't about to say no, not to Julia. Yes, she blew hot and cold – I couldn't read her at all – but I was going with the flow. Maybe I should've asked for her number, arranged to meet her some other time when she was less preoccupied, but I didn't. To be honest, by the time we were there, near the university, I was getting carried away by the whole idea. She had me wrapped round her little finger.'

'And?'

'That was as far as it went. Right here, she said, and I slowed the car, and there was someone standing outside her place. It was dark, and I couldn't be certain, but I got the feeling it was the kid she'd been fighting with earlier. You know, the same build and posture. Then I put my hand on her arm and she pushed it away. She was breathing so heavily I thought she was going to scream. I'm sorry, she said, I can't, there's someone I need to see, something I have to take care of. It was like – I don't know, I nearly lost my head at that, and grabbed her arm, but she pulled away and threw open the car door. Then she said, You don't understand, I can't expect you to understand, and she slammed the door in my face.' Dave gazed long and hard into his drink before emptying it. 'I almost went after her, but in the end I decided against it. Hell, I didn't much care any more what her game was, or who she was seeing, I just wanted out of there. She was too close to the edge, and I'd had my fill. So I fired up the engine and drove away, fast as I could. I didn't slow down until I was nearly home. Then I noticed Julia's shoe in the front passenger footwell. It must have come off when she scrambled out of the car, and she hadn't even thought to ask for it back. That's what happened and, Maggie, that's *all* that happened. I was angry at her, and when I got home I just dumped the shoe in the dustbin. *That* was a stupid thing to do, I know. On the news they said –'

'I know. I know what they said on the news.'

There was a lull between them then, a void filled with the drone of other people's chatter. Maggie took another brief sip of her wine – too chilled, too dry for her taste – and looked squarely at Dave Sessions. His face was an honest face, a face clouded with doubt and worry and confusion. Perhaps what he'd told her so far was true; it certainly seemed to plug several holes in the story as far as she knew it; but was that the whole story? Was there more?

She wanted, more than anything, to feel safe with him, but she couldn't, not yet, not with anyone. There were too many unanswered questions. Leaning across the table, she said, 'Thanks for telling me this, Dave. I still think you should tell the police. Maybe we should talk again soon.'

'You're going?' He looked startled. 'But you only just got here.'

'I have places to go. People to see. I'm only just getting started.'

'Then let me help. I could . . . At least I could give you a lift to wherever you're heading.'

She flinched at that. After the lift he'd given to Julia? That would be too much like replaying the past. 'I'll call you,' she said, touching his hand very briefly, very gently as she rose. Perhaps she would too, but not before this was finished, not before she knew who she could trust.

19

V was less busy than the night before, but she'd arrived at least one hour earlier. Still, there were dancers stomping beneath the flickering, mulitcoloured lights, and a growing crush at the bar. Squeezing in beside a burly, bearded man wearing a white T-shirt under his suit jacket, Maggie fumbled for her purse and waited her turn.

The man was wearing a cheap, tart aftershave that reminded her of unwanted Christmas gifts and filled her nostrils like burning rubber. As he searched his pockets for cash, then took out and set light to a cigarette, his elbow brushed firmly against her breasts. 'Excuse me,' she said, almost shouted, but he didn't seem to hear, didn't even glance her way. She was glad when he seized the beers he'd ordered and moved on, but the overpowering scent didn't leave with him. When the barman nodded at her, Maggie called for an Evian, then remembered too late what Linda had told her about the cost.

The water was £1.90, but she paid for it anyway. Hell, no one was forcing her to order another. From the balcony overlooking the stage, she stood picking out faces in the shifting light, swaying her hips to a Stone Roses song. Cradling her drink in both hands, she closed her eyes for a moment, half-dancing, hoping she looked suitably unselfconscious. She was here to have a good time, not spy on people, or at least that was the impression she needed to give. A little Dutch courage would go a long way – something stronger than spring water would soothe her – but she had to keep a clear head, now more than ever.

Maybe, Julia, maybe that's how *you* fell down, she thought. You had a few drinks here, probably one too many, and lowered your guard. For once, you didn't have your wits about you; you slacked off, you mistook the Angel of Death for Prince Charming.

There was no way Maggie would make the same mistake, no siree. She owed it to Julia not to foul up, not to follow her footsteps *all* the way, to a watery death. Of course, she could well understand why Linda and Christine would worry, but –

Linda and Christine. She glanced at her watch. She'd forgotten to call, and should have done so at least forty minutes ago. Perhaps the girls were now tearing their hair out, even summoning the police in a panic.

The ladies' room was upstairs. A red-carpeted stairwell took her there, leading from beneath a green neon sign at the far side of the dance floor. As she hurried upstairs, the thump-thump of techno – Sheep On Drugs – faded quickly, though the floor pounded under her feet as she rounded the top of the stairs, hurrying to the phone along a narrow, high-ceilinged corridor where the walls were dark red and gold velvet. The payphone hugged the wall just beyond the ladies' room.

'I'm fine,' she gasped before Linda could finish

reciting the number. 'I would've called earlier, but it completely slipped my mind. I'm sorry.'

'So you should be. And so much for your promises. Just wait till you get home.'

'I know, I know.'

'Is everything all right, Mags?'

'So far so good. Actually, it's been very uneventful so far.'

'Thank God; that's as it should be. When do you think you'll be done?'

'In a couple of hours, no later than midnight.'

'OK.' A brief lull. There were pips on the line. Then Linda said, 'Are you still alone?'

'Yes, but the night is young. Don't bother yourself; I still have my wits about me.'

'You'll need them. Take care of yourself. Oh, and Maggie?'

'Yes?' Maggie stalled the receiver, half-way to hanging it up.

'There's something you should know. Don't panic, but before you go any further –'

Her words were cut short as the last of Maggie's change ran out. The phone gave a metallic, impudent clunk, and that was that. She checked her purse for more coins, without luck. She must have used the rest of her silver at the bar.

Had an urgent note crept into Linda's voice at the very last minute, or had she imagined that? Surely, whatever Linda had said – tried to say – before the line went dead couldn't have been too vital; it had sounded like a warning, but anything so drastic wouldn't have slipped her mind until the call was almost over, would it?

Maggie hesitated by the phone, her fingers still gripping the dead receiver. She decided to call back, reversing the charges. Replacing and lifting the receiver again, she dialled the operator and waited. No more than a minute crawled by before she was connected; but the line was busy. 'I'll try again later,' she said, hanging up.

She was turning from the phone when a violent movement to her right made her start. The girl swaggering out of the ladies' room looked slightly the worse for drink, and, glaring at Maggie through sleepy pink eyes, she flung the door shut as heavy-handedly as she'd opened it, before sidling away to the stairs.

Maggie looked at the phone with a feeling of helplessness. Now, the floor underfoot was pounding so heavily it felt like her heart. From somewhere downstairs she heard a muffled scream, but it was only the singer of the song being played. When the screaming intensified, she hurried from the phone.

From the top of the stairwell the vocalist's words were still thick and obscure, as if he were singing underwater while drowning. *Don't panic*, Linda had said, inviting Maggie to do just that. Suddenly her nerves were shouting again, as if she'd downed too many cups of Linda's strong coffee. She ought to call the flat once more, but not from here, not from the trembling corridor where the colours were setting her nerves on edge.

Don't panic, but before you go any further –

She was hurrying now, taking the steps down the stairwell two at a time. It was only a momentary rush of adrenalin, and would pass in a minute or two. In a matter of hours she'd moved so much nearer to the truth about Julia than she'd ever imagined she would; and it scared her. But it was good to be fearful sometimes; fear kept you alert, on your guard, and she mustn't let her guard slip for one second because –

Maggie stopped in her tracks, half-way down. A man's silhouette was creeping around the curve in the stairwell below as he advanced up towards her. Down on the dance floor, one song melted into another, and now her heart really did feel in sympathy with its rhythm; unsteady and racing, out of control. She didn't have time to turn back, or even to think, before the silhouette filled the wall to her right and the figure became a person, became a face that she recognized but, right now, couldn't name.

'Julia,' he said, and then she knew.

20

She should have listened to the others. She should never have come here alone. They'd tried to warn her, and she'd been too pig-headed to care. Why? Was proving them wrong – proving how smart, how streetwise she was – really worth this hassle?

You're a fool, she scolded herself, a pig-headed, know-it-all fool. Just look at you now.

'Jesus, just look at you!' The voice startled her, cutting into her thoughts like a gunshot. 'You *could* pass for Julia, couldn't you? My God, I don't believe what I'm seeing.'

The stifled exclamation came from the figure on the stairs. Maggie's instincts told her to run, though her legs prevented her. Fear and indecision rooted her to the spot, trapping her like a deer in the path of car headlights.

'I don't believe it,' he repeated, taking another step upwards, surveying her as if she were a specimen in a glass cage. His face was clouded with confusion and wonder. 'Maggie, why on earth are you doing this?'

At last she breathed out. Even then, her heart tripped like a jackhammer, and in the last few seconds she'd grown so parched she feared she'd be unable to speak. 'You scared me,' she managed at last. 'Damn it all, Marcus, you half frightened the life out of me.'

He came up into the light, reaching for her arm. 'Well, maybe a good scare is exactly what you need. Do you really think this is wise, Maggie?'

'For a minute there I wasn't so sure. What are *you* doing here?'

'I ought to ask you the same question. Linda asked me to keep an eye on you. She and Christine seemed to think you needed help.'

'Do I look like I need help?'

'Frankly, yes. You're shaking all over.' He began steering her gently downstairs, gradually raising his voice as the music from V's dance floor boomed louder. 'They told me what you were up to, and that you wouldn't allow them to come. Linda thought that if I looked out for you –'

'A nice thought, but I don't need any help, thanks.'

'Yeah? Well, you've got it now, like it or not. It cost me a packet to get into this place and I'm not about to walk straight out again.'

They stalled before reaching the foot of the stairwell. To Maggie, Marcus appeared vaguely dishevelled and unshaven, as if he'd been woken from sleep to come here. Tonight he wore his long hair loose, without the pony-tail, and his eyes had a weary pink hue. He had on a plain grey T-shirt and a black denim waistcoat with leather trousers and boots. 'You want my opinion?' he said loudly.

'Not especially.'

'I think what you're doing is in very bad taste. Julia's gone and you're making it doubly hard on all the people who – who cared about her. In fact, I think what you're doing is sick.'

'I'm sorry that's how you see it. But this is what feels right to *me*, and besides, where's the alternative? Do you expect me to sit around mourning but doing nothing, like the rest of you?'

'No one expects you to mourn, because you never even knew her. And that's the whole point. Why the hell should this mean so much to you? Tell me that.'

She wished she could answer him clearly, coherently, but instead she shook her head, freeing her arm of his hold with a neat twist. 'Perhaps because I'm like her in so many ways,' she said, simply.

'Speak up, I can't hear for the music.'

'Never mind. It doesn't matter.'

'I'll tell you one thing for free.' Briefly, Marcus's eyes flared like torches. 'You're playing a very dangerous game, Maggie. You should let things be before you find yourself in serious trouble. They still haven't found Julia's killer, you know.'

'I'm aware of that. But if I can help things along –'

'Not like this, you can't. It'll be ten times worse if something happens to you too. Worse for your friends, worse for your folks, worse for the cops. Think about it. And if you weren't so – oh, to hell with it!' His voice peaked as he threw up his arms. Briefly, he looked so agitated she imagined he might throw her a punch. Then he relented, forcing a smile. 'Look, I'm sorry. You've had my opinion. There's no point in running it into the ground. I think you're mad, Maggie, but let me buy you a drink anyway, since I'm here.'

They sat at a table overlooking the dance floor with nothing between them but air and the thunder of a techno stomper that had customers idiot-dancing across the floor. Marcus glared into his beer, occasionally sneaking a glance in Maggie's direction as if the impulse to stare was too hard to resist. Despite his outburst, he still appeared strangely fascinated, as if Julia were there before him again. He made no attempt to talk, though, not even when a slower, mellower number by P.M. Dawn wafted from the sound system. Later, when Maggie suggested that he leave before her – she wouldn't be long – he shook his head stiffly and spoke his first words for almost an hour.

'I'm doing this for Linda, not you.'

That was when she decided to give in, at least for tonight. As long as Marcus was hovering, she had little hope of mingling with others who might know about Julia. 'Then let's go,' she said.

Outside, the city streets sparkled frostily. The winter air nipped at Maggie's legs as she hurried to keep pace with Marcus, and she wondered how Julia could ever have made a habit of dressing this way in this weather. Apart from a couple of drunks swaying on street corners and an occasional car breezing past, Briggate was deserted and quiet. The glittering pavement crisped underfoot like broken glass as they walked. Once or twice, Maggie thought she heard footsteps somewhere behind her, but when she spun around to look, there was no one.

'I'd better walk you home,' Marcus said. 'You've been nervous as a kitten all night.'

'Seeing you lurching up those stairs like something out of *Nosferatu* would've made anyone nervous.'

'*Lurch?* Me? I never *lurched* in my life.' Marcus stifled a laugh.

'Yes you did. Arms stretched out before you, fingers like talons . . .' Maggie clapped a hand to her mouth.

'God knows what was running through my mind. You must think I'm crazy.'

'Aren't you?'

'I don't think so. Not yet anyway.'

They walked on in silence for a time. As they reached Lower Briggate Marcus picked up the conversation. 'Well, I suppose *you* must think I'm pretty obnoxious, speaking to you the way I did.'

'Since you mention it . . .'

'No, seriously. Things haven't been easy since the first time we met. Not for me, not for anyone. I'm not usually like this, believe me.'

'I hope not.'

'Julia had quite an effect on everyone who knew her. She's left all of us in a state of shock.'

'Did you love her?' Maggie asked, remembering what Linda had said. The question was out before she could stop it.

Marcus looked at her askance; didn't speak again until they were crossing the bridge over the black, gleaming river. Then, slowing, he said, 'You know about us?'

'Doesn't everyone? Honestly, you can't expect me to live with *those* two blabbermouths without finding out. We girls share everything, even our secrets.'

'We were close for a while,' he said curtly. 'It was wrong, and we both knew it was wrong at the time, but it was one of those things we just couldn't stop. It was for Linda's sake that I finally called it off.'

'*You* called it off? But I thought –'

'Julia didn't take it too well, of course, but it was the only option I had. It was easy to fall under her spell – I wasn't the first – but Linda meant too much to me.

We've always had an understanding; we're right for each other, and I didn't want to sacrifice that.'

They had slowed to a halt, and were now standing at the bridge's midpoint, with city lights swimming and winking in the water like drowning stars. Again, Maggie felt a flutter of unease. Marcus stood facing her, shoulders heavy and sagging, a black caul of shadow concealing his features. He was supposed to be here to see her home safely; but suddenly she felt less than safe.

'Is that why Julia moved out?' she asked.

'No, I think she would've gone anyway. She and Hayden, this fiancé of hers down in Cambridge, had been going through a rocky time together, the kind of thing that happens when you're at college, miles apart; and I think that's why Julia threw herself at me, on the rebound. Everything had to be now, now, now. She needed to be on a constant high. After we broke up and then Linda came home, there wasn't too much to keep her.'

'I see.' They began walking again, and Maggie was relieved when the streetlights further ahead washed over his face again. 'Did Linda find it easy to forgive you?'

'Not easy, no, but how could she? We'd betrayed her, and we were supposed to be special people in her life. Truth be told, Julia was a very bad influence. It was very hard to resist her, even when I knew how much damage I'd cause.'

'But you gave her every opportunity, Marcus. Don't pretend you were innocent, because you weren't. You had a choice, but you let yourself get sucked in.'

'I'm not sure I want to talk any more,' he murmured.

They were nearing the streets which led to the flat. Here, the buildings were red-brick terraces, dark and blank and silent. A handful of living-room lights flared behind lace curtains, but the quiet made Maggie hurry, heels clattering noisily.

'I guess you could say that Julia helped us, as things turned out,' Marcus said. 'What happened could've destroyed me and Linda, but in the end it brought us closer. We understand each other now in ways we really couldn't before. But, yes, I miss Julia; of course I do. Sometimes . . .' His voice faded to a whisper as they rounded a corner and the flat came into view. 'Sometimes I wake up feeling certain she's still alive. I can smell her, almost see her. And then I remember, and it kills me, it really does. So when I saw you tonight –'

'You called me Julia,' she said.

'I did?' he sounded astonished. They were passing beneath a streetlight, and in the amber glow his features seemed almost like a child's; pinched and tight-lipped, as if he were forcing himself not to weep. 'You *are* so alike,' he said dreamily. 'That's what's so scary, because it's as if you've brought her back, which you shouldn't have done, because it *is* over, and she *has* gone, and none of us wants to go through that nightmare again.'

'I'm sorry,' she said. 'I didn't mean to upset anyone. I'm doing this for other reasons. There's so much I still need to know . . .'

Marcus forced a smile, not looking at her but at the upstairs windows of the house. 'The lights are out,' he said quietly. 'I suppose the others are asleep by now.'

'They have classes tomorrow.'

He gave a faint nod.

'You're welcome to come in for coffee,' she said.

'Not tonight. I'd better be getting back. Thanks anyway.'

'And thanks for walking me home.'

Suddenly, without warning, he reached for her hand, drawing her slowly towards him. 'Sorry if I've been disagreeable, Maggie. It's nothing personal, honestly. You should see me on a better day.'

'There'll be better days soon,' she said. 'I know so. Just wait.' He was easing her closer, inch by inch, and while her instincts told her to pull back, break loose of his hold, she didn't resist. The next thing she knew his arms were around her, his lips brushing her cheek.

'Good-night,' he said. 'It's OK. Christine always gets a good-night kiss too. It doesn't mean anything.'

Of course it didn't. It didn't mean a thing. But for one fleeting moment she understood only too well what Julia had seen in him. The sultry good looks, the offbeat dress sense, the darkness behind his eyes were strangely, compulsively magnetic. There was more to Marcus than brawn and bad temper, and at once she found herself wanting more.

A picture of Ian flashed on and off in her mind, like a slideshow snapshot, as he forced himself closer, his kisses straying from her cheek to her mouth. It's been such a long time, she thought absently. So long, too long. She needed someone, and her lips were parted and ready for him; she braced herself as his groin pressed firmly against hers. She was losing herself in Marcus's arms, and the circle was complete. It was beginning again. She was alive and on fire. It wasn't until his icy fingers skirted inside her jacket to cup her left breast that she awoke, remembering who she was and who *he* was. Then she was untangling herself from his arms, stumbling backwards, flinging out both her hands to keep him at bay.

'No, Marcus! No!' Her voice was nearer a hiss than a shout. 'We can't. *I* can't . . .'

'What's wrong with you?' Beneath the streetlight his face seemed clear and expressionless. 'What did you think I was doing?'

'Think? I *know* what you were doing.' Everything he'd told her on the way here meant nothing. She couldn't believe a word he'd said. He'd betrayed Linda before and would do so again; he couldn't be trusted. Yes, there was a darkness about him, an attractive darkness, but dangerous too.

'I – I have to go now.' She turned, began crossing the street, hurrying in case he decided to follow. Her head felt crammed with chattering, insane voices. As she reached the front door, slammed her key in the lock and budged the door open, he called after her, and his words turned her heart to stone.

'Goddamn you, you're all the same,' Marcus said.

So are you, she thought, unable to reply; her throat felt tired and cramped. So are you. So are you.

21

She slept in fits and starts. At two, three-thirty and
five in the morning she found herself wide awake,
staring at the gap in the curtains as though half-
expecting to see Julia peering in. A murmur of distant
thunder didn't help – she never slept easily during
storms – but weather was the least of her problems
right now. Marcus had set a trap for her, and like a
fool she'd stepped neatly into it. How stupid could you
get?

It was only a moment of weakness, everyone had
weaknesses, but this was too close, too much like the
past replaying itself. Last night she'd lost herself; she'd
let down her guard . . . And you could never afford to let
down your guard, *never*. And when Marcus kissed her –

He was kissing Julia, right? He was touching *her*,
kissing *her*, not you, she thought.

Goddamn you, you're all the same.

What on earth would Linda say when she heard
about this? Of course, she would have to be told; there
was no sense in hiding the truth. Besides, Maggie
thought, we girls *do* share everything, even our secrets.
And when we have secrets we can't keep them for
long; we're like Geiger counters, us. We know when
something's wrong. We can read one another.

She rose just before six, stirred a spoonful of honey into a mug of hot milk, which she took back to bed and sipped, lost in thought, with the pillows fluffed up behind her. You're just a frustrated wreck, she scolded herself. You opened yourself up to Marcus just because he was *there*; no other reason. Bad move. Very bad move. Well, who needs him? And who needs Ian? Who needs any of them? Look where it gets you. Look where it got *Julia*, for crying out loud. If you must play the great detective, at least have the good sense to follow your head, not your sex, dummy.

Because sex wasn't the only attraction here, was it? Sure, if Julia had taught her anything it was that she, Maggie Waverly, wasn't just some dumpy, ugly kid with no prospects; she had plenty to offer, could turn heads with the best of them, and needn't be afraid any more. But this was more about being confident, being strong enough to say no. Julia *had* let something loose in her, something new and marvellous and scary, but she still had the power, the strength to say no.

Maggie shivered and tugged up the bedsheets.

Sister Hyde, indeed!

But you've had so little and she had so much, she thought, placing the empty mug on her bedside table. You've never had that kind of life. And suddenly, like Julia, you want it all at once.

Still restless, she didn't even bother trying to sleep again. She showered, dressed and breakfasted by seven, and sometime before eight found herself standing outside the library, key in hand, one and a half hours before opening time. It was ridiculously early, but she wouldn't be able to relax in the flat; she needed to keep herself occupied.

Letting herself in, she collected the morning papers and folded them on to their racks in the readers' room. In the small kitchenette off the library's main floor, she made tea, which she brought to the counter. It cooled at her elbow while she rummaged in her bag, Julia's bag, for the address book. Suddenly she knew what she had to do. She took a deep breath before dialling the number Julia had listed beside Hayden's name.

The male voice that answered, after a wait that felt like minutes, sounded slow and disorientated. 'Hello?'

'I'm sorry if I woke you. Is Hayden there?'

'Nnnn . . . What time is this? What day? Did you say Hayden? Well, he isn't here. Who wants him?'

'The name's Maggie Waverly. I was – I was a friend of Julia's.' Silence. 'Do you have his number in Cambridge?'

'Sure, but . . . you won't find him there.'

'But he's studying in Cambridge, isn't he?'

'*Was* studying there, but . . . Listen, if you knew Julia you'll know the whole story by now.'

'I'm sorry. She didn't tell me everything.'

'She didn't tell you he quit his course after they broke up?'

Maggie felt a slow, cold sensation burrowing under her skin. But they were going to marry; that's what she'd intended, wasn't it? 'I don't understand,' she said faintly.

'You must know. They were never any good for each other, if you want my opinion; it was just the wrong chemistry, whatever you want to call it. When they split, Hayden took a backpack to the continent to get his head straight. He's still over there now, as far as I know. Shall I ask him to call you if I hear from him soon?'

'No. No, that's all right.' She hung up without thanking the man for his time.

OK, this was news, but what kind of news, and could she believe it anyway? 'You're full of surprises, Julia,' she said, snapping the address book shut, dropping it into the bag. 'How many more before we're through? How many?' Mystified, she sat with a pencil and paper, doodling.

Marcus? she wrote. Then, *Hayden? Dave Sessions? Scott? Ian??*

Suspects all.

No, not necessarily all.

Ian hadn't necessarily known Julia, though she was angry enough with him not to rule him out so soon. Nor could she rule out Dave Sessions, no matter how sincere he'd seemed over drinks at Harvey's. Hayden? The others had known her, or at least crossed her path. One way or another she'd had a dramatic effect on all of them; but enough to drive one of them to murder?

Mr X? she wrote, meaning someone unknown. It was a fair bet that the killer could yet prove to be a wild card, a stranger. It was easy to suspect those you already knew, but how many other lives had Julia touched? Maggie put down the pencil and frowned at the psychology section for inspiration.

Then she snatched up the pencil again, and wrote: *Patrick Carver.* Of course: how could she have overlooked him? After his little exhibition in here only yesterday, the train-spotter ought to be top of her list. There was a new, distant grumble of thunder as she switched on the computer and began scrolling through a list of library members. She'd assumed the thunder had gone by in the night; the storm hadn't actually broken but passed on before dawn. Perhaps this time the rain would come, bringing cleaner air in its path. She hoped so – in spite of the cold the atmosphere this morning seemed unusually heavy for late October.

Boorman, Brook, Bryce and Butterfield rolled up her screen like credits at the end of a film. Please let him be on the list! It would be just her luck if he'd somehow escaped the register, or had changed his name and address without informing the library. There were serious questions she needed to ask Mr Carver. As she worked through the list something flashed, bright as a floodlight, outside the library's entrance. Maggie glanced at the street, but the brightness had already passed; the morning light seemed squeezed and grey and the thunder, ten seconds later, sounded louder and closer than before. When she returned to the screen, her forefinger still jamming down the scroll key, she realized she'd skipped past the train-spotter's details. Here it came, though. Scrolling up, she watched the screen credits roll in reverse. Campbell, Carrick, Carson . . .

Carver. She looked at his name several times. Something was wrong. Something was definitely, seriously wrong. It took her almost a minute to fully digest it.

She had to be mistaken, too weary to read the screen properly. Either that or she'd lost her senses completely, because the address on the screen next to Carver's name was her own: post code, street name, house number . . . everything. Maggie blinked and looked again. The only difference she could see was his flat number, two.

All right, she thought. Steady on, breathe deeply. What you're seeing is an address, nothing more. Don't lose your head. Think.

But why hadn't she noticed him coming and going from the house? Surely *he* had seen her. But if he had, then why hadn't he mentioned it? He wouldn't have let it pass: Um, er, Miss Waverly, you know something funny? It's such a small world, so it is!

Maggie sat back and took a sip of her tea, hardly tasting it. She'd wanted to confront Patrick Carver about yesterday; his clumsy hints and half-warnings still bothered her. She could still hear his voice – 'You have to be careful . . . It would be terrible if the same thing happened to you' – merging with all the others inside her head.

OK, she thought. Take your time; don't be rash. She still had an hour before Joyce Durham and Kate Bradshaw were due to arrive for work; time enough to slip home again, hammer on the train-spotter's door until he answered, demand to know what he knew. Maybe he'd fall into line if she promised to go to the police unless he talked. He'd seemed in such a dreadful hurry to escape her yesterday; but by then the damage was done – he'd already told Maggie more than he meant to, enough to make her suspicious.

Thunder brooded over the streets as she stepped outside, locking the library door after her. The key jarred slightly in the lock, which must have grown rusty in the recent wet weather. By the time she reached the bridge over the river, the sky had darkened considerably and the first drops of rain were patting the tarmac. Half-way across the bridge, a picture of Marcus, his features obscured by darkness, leapt into her mind. He was speaking to her, but the words weren't his own, they belonged to a girl, the girl with the felt hat in the coffee shop. 'Believe me, Julia wasn't an angel,' the voice was ranting. 'Ask your friends, why don't you? Ask them what she was *really* like.'

Maggie blinked the spectre away, picking up her step towards home. An underfed mongrel dog raised its head from a swollen, black dustbin bag, growling, as she turned into her street. The streetlights were dying, one by one, and when she came within sight of the flat, the open curtains at the window told her the girls were up and about.

At first she couldn't understand why the door wouldn't open when she fitted the key. Some half-wit must have used the bolt. Then she realized the key in her hand was the library's. Slow *down*, breathe deeply, don't get ahead of yourself. Inserting her own key, she stepped inside.

A pile of mail scuffed under her feet as she closed the door firmly behind her. A rack of six numbered pigeon-holes hung on the wall to her right. These were scrawled in black ink on white slivers of paper, overlaid with Sellotape. She put the mail on top, not bothering to sort it, before moving into the gloomy hall. There were two doorways here: Flat One on her immediate left, Flat Two further along the hall, half-hidden by shadows under the stairs. A single unshaded bulb hung from the ceiling between them. She'd reached Carver's door and was preparing to knock, when the first doubts crept over her, freezing her fist in mid-flight.

Suppose the train-spotter *does* know something?

Suppose he knows more than you *want* to know? Suppose he's dangerous? You could disappear into his flat and never be heard from again.

She really ought to alert the others. That was the sensible thing to do. As long as someone knew where she was and what she had in mind, she could proceed. Maybe she could even drag Linda and Christine along for company. Then, later, they could confirm anything the train-spotter might tell her to the police, if necessary.

She was turning away, towards the stairs, when a sudden flurry of movement behind the door stopped her again. There was the sound of a bolt being pulled back, a key being turned and, before she could jump clear, the door swung fully open. A scrawny pale man in his late fifties or early sixties, with dishevelled, thinning grey hair and piercing grey eyes, peered out at her from the doorway, stifling a yawn. He was only half-dressed, with his grubby white shirt unbuttoned to the waist, the braces of his trousers sagging to his knees.

'Thought I heard something,' he said. 'What's going on?'

'I'm looking for a Mr Carver. Patrick Carver,' Maggie said.

'Well, here I am,' the man said, rubbing sleep from his eyes. 'What can I do for you, miss?'

22

Nothing was quite what it seemed, Maggie knew. If nothing else, the last few days had taught her not to take anything at face value. Even so, the old man had caught her totally off balance, and she didn't know what to say. She looked at him in bewilderment, mouth agape. He returned the look, blinking, yawning.

'You're not him,' she said feebly. 'You're not Patrick Carver, are you?'

'I should know well enough who I am, young lady. Why would I claim to be someone I'm not?'

'I'm sorry.' She backed off a little. 'I was expecting someone much younger.'

'Sorry to disappoint you.' She was edging along the hall towards the foot of the stairs when he took one slow step past the threshold and called after her, raising his voice a little, 'Wait a minute. The Patrick Carver you're looking for, what's he look like?'

'So tall, so wide.' She made futile gestures with her hands which only seemed to confuse him. 'And kind of sheepish-looking. He wears glasses, dresses in grungy charity-shop clothes and –'

'Go no further,' the man said abruptly. At first she thought he meant that literally; up the stairs, out of his reach. But his face had slackened, a skewed smile overtaking his lips. 'You're thinking of our Carl, that's who. You've got his name muddled up, though.'

'He's your son?'

'Stepson. His surname isn't Carver, either. It's Bryce, from his mother's first marriage.'

'Ah.' Maggie found herself relaxing slightly. 'Is he home?'

'Doesn't live here any more. Nor does the old girl herself, for that matter. I've had my lot with the both of them, tell you the truth. There must be something bad in their bloodstream, that family, they don't appreciate anything you do for them. Work your fingers to the bone . . .' He was leaning against the door-frame, scratching his scalp with fingernails that looked dirty and stained even from several feet away. 'Still, you don't want to hear my life story. The short and the tall is that *she's* gone off with some new fancy man with a flash car and *he's* in digs somewhere up near the university, or was the last I heard. He drops in from time to time on the scrounge, when he needs something. He wouldn't show his face out of the kindness of his heart, that's for sure.'

'I see.'

'Bloody waste of space, that kid. I'm better off without both of them, I swear.'

'Do you have his current address?'

'Somewhere abouts. It's on Woodhouse Lane, I can tell you that much. I saw the place once, a typical student dump; falling apart from the floorboards up. Just wait a minute.'

Maggie waited while the real Patrick Carver ducked inside the flat, emerging some two or three minutes later with a scrap of lined notepaper across which he'd scrawled the address in a large, looping hand. 'Will that do you?'

'It's fine. Thank you.'

'How come he gave you my name instead of his own?' he asked. 'Is the brat trying to give me a bad reputation or something?'

Maggie shrugged. 'I'm not sure he ever gave a name. I assumed he was Patrick Carver because that's what it said on his library ticket. I work at the branch near the wharf,' she explained.

'Well, there you go. Like I said, he only comes down here when he wants something. He probably borrowed my ticket one time when he couldn't find his and couldn't be bothered to apply for another. Nothing that failure borrows ever comes back. There's no such thing as a loan, where he's concerned.'

'Then I ought to be grateful he returned his library books,' Maggie said. 'Thanks very much, Mr Carver.'

He raised a hand as he retreated inside. The door closed, the key turned, the bolt slammed, and Maggie started upstairs. As she stepped into the flat, Christine screamed and Linda covered her O of a mouth with a hand.

'You lousy rat bag,' Christine said.

'That's a fine welcome, I must say. What happened to good-morning? I liked that a lot better.'

'We've been going to pieces over you,' Linda complained. 'Where on earth have you been? I thought . . . We both thought . . .'

'You didn't come home last night,' Christine said. A huge sigh of relief escaped her as she lowered herself, a fragile shell, on to the couch. 'And there was no sign of you when we got up this morning. No message. No nothing.'

'We were on the verge of calling the police,' Linda said. 'Where *were* you?'

Maggie, finally catching her breath, closed the door and tugged off her coat. 'Jesus, it's good to know you care, but I *was* here. I came home late, that's all, but didn't sleep too well and decided to leave early for work. I didn't think –'

'No, you didn't think.' Christine was shaking her head, pursing her lips. 'We told you before you went out last night how we hated the idea, didn't we?'

'But you sent Marcus along to protect and defend me.'

Linda gave a dry laugh. 'Right. You can blame Christine for *that* particular brainwave. I'll bet the hopeless louse couldn't even *find* you.'

'Hear how she talks about the one she loves?' Christine smirked. 'God help her enemies, is all I can say. How went the evening anyway, Mags?'

'Strangely. I'll tell you about it later.' She didn't want to discuss Marcus yet, not until her mind had cleared; for one thing, she hadn't the slightest idea how to begin, how to assure Linda about what had happened.

Casting her coat on to an armchair, she took Linda's arm, steering her on to the couch beside Christine. 'I'm sorry about this morning, really I am. I should've left you a note, or at least called from the library.'

'What brought you back?' Linda asked.

'Ah, yes. Remember the guy we were talking about? The one who Julia said was following her?'

'The train-spotter?'

'The very same. Didn't I tell you he uses the

library? When I checked his address, it led me right to this building, to one of the flats downstairs.'

'You're kidding.' Linda's eyes widened. 'How come we never see him around?'

'That crossed my mind too. It turns out his father lives there, or rather his stepfather does. The guy – Carl Bryce – had been using the wrong library ticket, is all. But I have his current address. The old guy downstairs just gave it to me.'

'And what do you propose to do with it?' Christine wondered, alarmed. 'If you think the train-spotter is so suspicious, why not just report him to the police?'

'I'd like to talk to him first. I think he may know something. That's why –'

'You're getting out of your depth, aren't you, sis?' Linda said. 'Last night was bad enough. But if you're going to carry on with this insane investigation, we'll *all* be nervous wrecks by the time you're done.'

'I need your help.' Maggie's gaze flitted from Linda to Christine. 'If you'll both come along there won't be any trouble, I'm certain. The guy seems more scared than scary to me.'

'Count me out.' Linda was adamant. She was shaking her head in short, stiff, robotic movements; her posture was rigid and tense. 'This is police business, and if Carl whatever-his-name-is has a story to tell, let him tell it to *them*. If he's innocent he'll go to the law himself, of his own free will. And while he's about it, the rest of us can get on with our lives.' Suddenly she clasped Maggie's hand with both her own. 'Leave it alone, Mags. Let it rest. Let *Julia* rest.'

There was a prolonged, uneasy silence before Christine said, 'Count me in, Mags. Hell, I'll go with you.

If you can't beat 'em join 'em, right? Besides, you'd go ahead with or without us, wouldn't you?'

'Yes, I would.'

'You're nuts, but I'll help if I can.' Christine gave Linda a nudge in the ribs. 'I always said she was nuts, didn't I? Loopy as a lemming.'

'You both are. We should never have offered her that room,' Linda agreed, smiling faintly, her shoulders still rigid with tension. 'I *knew* she'd be more trouble than she's worth.'

Maggie glanced at the window, drawn by another double flash of lightning. Thunder followed almost immediately. The storm had arrived. 'See you there at one,' she said, unfolding the scrap of lined paper from her jeans and passing it to Christine. 'I'll meet you outside.' Jumping to her feet, she collected her coat from the armchair and marched to the door. 'Are you sure you're OK about this?'

'Shut up and go.' Christine waved her away. 'I'll be there. Someone has to look out for you. It's obvious *you* don't know how to.'

23

The phone call came just after twelve, while Maggie
was returning paperbacks to their display racks in the
fiction section. Kate called her to the desk, and when
she took up the phone Christine said, 'Mags? About
Carl Bryce. I've got to take a rain-check. Sorry, but
they've scheduled an extra class for this morning. I'll
not be away until two. That's too late for you, I
suppose.'

'I have to be back here before then. Never mind.
I'll –'

'Make it tomorrow then, or some other time; after
you finish work, let's say. As long as you don't go
alone.' Christine sounded fragile and nervous. 'You're
not going to do anything foolish, are you?'

'Don't worry. You know me.'

'That's why I *am* worried. Don't think I can't see
what's happening to you, Mags. I realize how caught
up in all this you must feel, especially since the police
reconstruction, but that doesn't mean you have to go
looking for trouble.'

'I'm not. I want to talk to him, that's all.'

'I wish . . .' Christine's voice collapsed to a weary
sigh. 'I wish we'd never got you started on this kick, I
really do.'

'Which kick is that?'

'Dressing yourself up like Julia. Trying to get under her skin, to make yourself like her. You were acting, the other night, remember; there's no need to take it further than that.'

'I hear you. And if it makes you feel any easier, I'm too big a wimp to take stupid risks. I'm aware that this isn't a game.'

'Then promise me one thing. Promise me you'll not go alone.'

'I can't say that. But I wouldn't even consider it if I thought it was dangerous.'

'Then why did you ask me to go in the first place? You can't have it both ways, Mags.' A rapid succession of pips on the line forced Christine to stall for a moment. Then she said, 'Look, I'm out of coins and the class is about to start. Let's talk about this later, because if you –'

The line went dead as the last of Christine's change was swallowed up. Maggie recradled the receiver, hovering over it until certain Christine wouldn't call back. Yes, she *did* want it both ways, but she'd already made it clear that she'd go ahead with or without the others. In any case, the train-spotter might be an oddball, but he didn't strike fear into her heart; he hadn't said or done anything remotely threatening.

The storm had faded to a light sprinkle of rain by the time she signed off for lunch, stepped outside into air that was pleasantly cool and breathable again and strolled up to City Square in search of a bus. The wet streets gleamed about her; traffic surged past the railway station in a mindless stream, showering pedestrians on Wellington Street as they waited to cross. A flicker of lightning in a doorway opposite the bus stand on Infirmiry Street made Maggie wonder where she'd left her umbrella, but the flash was more like a glint of sunlight on glass.

The bus ride took less than ten minutes, but before it was over she was wishing she'd decided to walk. A small yellow poster of Julia at the front of the bus faced the seated passengers, many of whom spent the journey to Woodhouse Lane ogling her. One white-haired woman, seated across the aisle from Maggie, opened her toothless mouth to speak, then thought better of it as Maggie got up to hit the bell. A small fat-faced boy smirked and pointed his finger as she fumbled past his seat to the doors.

'What's *your* problem?' she asked quietly.

'You're dead,' the boy leered. 'Bang, bang!'

Jesus, she didn't need to dress up to feel she was carrying Julia with her wherever she went. Her face was burning by the time she'd clambered outside and the doors had wheezed shut behind her. While the bus lurched away along Woodhouse Lane, she crossed to the row of shops opposite the University campus. A newsagent's, a baker's and a hairdresser's salon stood shoulder to shoulder between two narrow junctions. There was also a disco near by, judging by the deafening rap music she could hear – but the noise came from the hairdresser's, whose doors were wide open to the street.

Inside, the assistants looked like cloned models; two girls with bleached-blonde hair and beauty-salon tans and two boys with weight-training physiques wafted scissors, combs and mirrors about the heads of four vacant-eyed clients in strait-jackets.

'I'm looking for number 242, Flat B,' Maggie called from the door, into the fog of noise.

The girl nearest her looked up from a client's permed beehive with a quizzical frown. 'Huh?'

'Number 242. Flat B.' This time she mouthed the words slowly.

The girl's face cleared. 'Up there.' With a quick, impatient jab of her curling tongs at the ceiling, she returned to work.

There was another, unnumbered door next to the hairdresser's. The red glossy paint had become flaky and dull with age and sun. On the wall beside the door was a row of three buzzers, also nameless and numberless. Presumably Flat B was the middle one, but no one answered when she pressed it, and after two minutes no one had come to the door. She pressed it again, then tested the door with a gentle push.

It sighed gently open before her. Soon she was standing in a dim, bombed-out-looking hallway with a bare concrete floor, flaking grey paintwork and air that felt thick with dust. A line of rubbish bags stood along the base of one wall. Music from the hairdresser's next door boomed like a party in the narrow, echoic space. People *live* here? she wondered. People can actually *stand* to live here?

Maggie moved along the hall to the stairs on her left, the grimy floor scuffing and scraping underfoot. The first flight of stairs were bare wood, and the hollow clump of her shoes when she started up seemed embarrassingly loud, as if she were climbing on horseback. At least the first floor was carpeted, even if its swirling, brightly coloured pattern was sufficient to give her a headache. There was a smell of new paint, and underlying that a tart, bitter scent, as if someone wearing cheap perfume had passed this way not long ago. To her right, at the turn of the stairs, was a dirt-streaked window overlooking the street. To her left, along the landing, were the doors to two flats, both painted white. The first, on the building's Woodhouse Lane side, was Flat A. The next one along was Carl Bryce's, then.

Maggie made a bee-line for his door, but hesitated when she reached it. Maybe she'd come too far too soon. It was one thing to ask to talk to him, quite another to storm his home uninvited. In any case, he wasn't at home, or he would have answered the buzzer – problem solved. Unless, of course, his buzzer was out of order. Bracing herself, Maggie gave the door a timid tap, and waited.

Again, silence answered her.

What she did then was something she'd never imagined she could. Before she could think it through, she'd seized the door-knob, given it one firm twist, and pushed the door open.

Fully open. He'd left the damn place unlocked. Who, in this day and age, was stupid enough to leave *anything* unlocked? Inside she could see the cluttered living-room: a shabby, two-piece suite, a coffee table littered with magazines, a small TV set perched on a plastic kitchen chair.

'Anyone home?' Maggie called, weakly. 'Mr Bryce, are you there?'

Still no answer. Time to go home, or back to work, or *anywhere* away from here. That's what any sensible person would do, right? But she'd moved far beyond being sensible lately. She'd entered another world altogether, a world of glamour, risk and discovery. She was following her nose, almost as if someone else – someone without her own good sense – were guiding her. She could almost feel Julia pushing, coaxing, whispering words of encouragement: Go on, go ahead, you want to know, don't you? Take a step through this door and you're one step nearer. Trust me, trust me.

'Shut up,' Maggie replied. Talking to oneself was the first sign of madness, they said, and it would be madness to set even one foot inside this place; as good as breaking and entering. Then, while her mind – the smart and sensible part of her mind – was withdrawing, turning, racing downstairs again, the rest of her strode calmly into the flat and closed the door.

That's it, she thought. You just crossed the line. Whatever happens now is your own responsibility, you can't pretend you haven't been warned. At first glance the flat seemed larger than she'd expected, but just as untidy. Carl Bryce had never struck her as a nit-picking, house-proud type; not that the room was filthy: he just hadn't bothered with little household chores like straightening cushions and magazines, clearing away cups still half-filled with cold liquid. A couple of framed, novelty photo prints hung askew on the walls: a line of penguins leaping into the sea from a jutting rock; a whale's tail breaking the ocean's surface. At least his taste in art was a pleasant relief. After the books he'd borrowed from the library she'd expected to find Hieronymus Bosch hanging here, or Hannibal Lecter at *least*.

Photography seemed to be his thing, in fact. Most of the magazines were photo monthlies, and a Pentax SLR camera and several rolls of film lolled in an armchair before the TV. On the other side of the room, beneath the window, a small Formica table doubled as a desk. A portable typewriter sat on top of it. Loose papers cluttered the space around it; some lay scattered on the floor. To the right of the desk was a grey filing cabinet. Three of its drawers were wide open. The papers inside were a disorganized rat's nest, as if Bryce had been rummaging through them for something he'd lost.

OK, she'd come this far, but what now? Did she search cupboards and drawers? She was here to talk, not pry. Even so, she found herself drifting from the lounge, along a short dim corridor, past two doors, to the kitchen, and the lingering smell of burnt toast.

The sink was a dumping-ground of greasy, unwashed pans, plates and cups. Through the window above it was a view of the back streets. The houses were huge, red Victorian piles. Every dark window looked as though it might hold some terrible secret. At the centre of the bare-boarded floor was a dining table on which Carl Bryce had plonked his college work – a large, black, box file and a notebook and pens – and a couple more dirty plates for good measure. Good grief, even Linda and Christine were better housekeepers than this!

She clumped to the table and sat for a moment, hesitating before opening the file. The first three pages of spidery notes were headed *Crime and Delinquency*; *The Criminal Mind*; *Roots and Causes of Anti-social and Sociopathic Behaviour*.

At least the train-spotter was as good as his word on that score. He *had* been studying this stuff, not getting off on it. For some reason this made her feel easier.

She wasn't necessarily dealing with a liar – just a guy who knew something, who'd seen something. She skimmed a few more pages at leisure. *Peer Groups*, *Wealth*, *Income*, *Social Policy*. More of the same. Then, half-way through the file, Maggie came to a dead halt. Here was a page – two pages – of hastily written notes almost lost in a ream of blank sheets. Having speed-read the first paragraph, she began again, slowly, heart in mouth.

This had nothing to do with his studies, unless he was also taking a course in fiction. But this wasn't fiction. It was something else again; something she was almost afraid to identify, an extract from some kind of diary. Whatever came before this was missing, however, and the spidery handwriting began in mid-sentence:

– how she'll react when I tell her you're mine, you'll always be mine. I'm telling her this for the last time but again she refuses to listen. I tell her how much she means to me but she pulls away with this poisonous look in her eyes. Says terrible things to me. Says things you wouldn't believe a beautiful girl like her ever could. You'd think when you saw her she could only ever be as sweet and graceful on the inside as she is on the outside, but appearances can deceive. You can't judge a book by its cover. For a second I've got this picture in my head of a Venus Flytrap – scented, pretty to look at but deadly. I wish I could explain this to her, but I'm not sure she'd really understand.

So after a minute or two of standing around she says good-bye and good luck. I don't want you following me again. Stay where you are or I swear

I'll call the police. So leave me alone. Why can't
everyone just leave me alone? That's when I lose
control and make a grab for her. Can't help myself
– I just have this overpowering need to hold her
close, even if she hates me, because I know that if I
can touch her just for a moment it'll make everything
all right; she'll perhaps hate me less or understand
that I don't mean any harm. But when I move
towards her –

Maggie broke off there, covering the page with both
hands. The words were making her skin crawl – surely
he was describing Julia, even if she wasn't mentioned
by name; Bryce must have known her, and known her
well – but that wasn't the reason she'd stopped
reading.

It was something she'd heard. A car door had
slammed on the street below. From the kitchen window
she could see only a bottle-green Triumph, and a
reedy, stiff-limbed old man climbing out of it. No need
to panic. She doubted Carl Bryce could afford to run a
car, and he'd probably be in lectures all day. But
would he have gone without his file, even if he'd
forgotten to lock up the flat? No one could be *that*
neglectful.

In any case, it was time she was leaving. The little
she'd read so far had given her a case of the shakes,
and she didn't care to be here if he *did* return. She
would read the rest later, in a safer place. Before
leaving the kitchen, she folded the pages into her bag,
then closed the file.

These notes could be the key to everything, but she
mustn't dwell on them now. All she had to do was beat

a careful retreat, keep her nerve for another two minutes until she was clear of the building. She strode
from the kitchen, past the door on her left marked
Bathroom, then faltered. The next door along was
open a couple of inches; and there was someone behind
it, she was certain.

'Hello?' Her voice was a cracked, dry whisper
through which she could hear herself wanting to shout.
She gave the door a light tap. 'I know someone's in
there. Mr Bryce?'

Then, hardly daring to breathe, she pushed the door
wide open – and her heart nearly stopped.

Julia stared back at her from all four walls. There
was no one else here; only Julia. A hundred Julias.
Perhaps two hundred. Possibly more.

The room – Bryce's bedroom – was south-facing,
and the light streaming in through the uncurtained
window was easily sufficient to see by, even though the
sky was still dark. The train-spotter's unmade bed
stood headboard first against the right-hand wall.
Above, and to either side of it, were small, snapshot-
sized colour prints of Julia, tacked so closely together
they overlapped at the edges. The facing wall was
almost entirely covered with more of them. So was the
wall by the window.

Jesus, what *was* this? What *had* he been up to?

Leaving the door open, she took a step into the
room, which suddenly felt like a shrine, a hallowed
place where people spoke in low, respectful tones as
they viewed the exhibits. Well, these particular exhibits
were enough to provoke screaming, not whispers.
Maggie stared at them, one hand pressed to her mouth,
just in case. None of the shots seemed to have been

taken with Julia's knowledge. Many were blurry and out of focus. Most were taken from a distance, sometimes with soft shapes in the foreground – a pedestrian's shoulder, the wing mirror of a car – while Julia crossed a street, or window-gazed, or ate ice-cream while shielding her eyes from the sun.

You're spying on a spy, Maggie thought. Carl Bryce had been following Julia, just as she'd claimed. She hadn't been paranoid, but she had been wise enough, aware enough not to let her imagination run riot. In many of the snaps Julia had a natural, easy beauty that Maggie envied, a beauty she clearly hadn't bothered to work at: her hair was ragged and unbrushed, her clothes draped loosely and casually about her as if she'd just thrown them on as an afterthought. In others, taken by night, she looked more carefully groomed, with a hint of lip gloss or eyeliner to highlight her features.

Here was one in which she wore the black dress. She perched at a table in a bustling courtyard outside a café or bar, sipping a tall, dark drink through a straw. She was alone, again unaware of the camera. Her legs were visible, crossed at the ankle under the table, and she was wearing slim, heel-less black shoes to match the dress, one of which she'd left in Dave Sessions' white Fiesta. You look so sad, Maggie thought, moving closer. Julia must have had everything she needed in life, but you wouldn't have thought so to see her like this. Her eyes were glazed and far away, her lips pursed. She seemed close to tears.

Maggie decided to keep this shot. The police ought to know what she'd found, and they should talk to Carl Bryce, if they hadn't already. Of course, they'd rap her knuckles when she explained how she'd come by the print, but one quick scan of this flat and they'd know who the real culprit was. Tugging the photograph free of the wall, she slipped it into her bag, alongside the pages of the diary. Then, casting one last glance at the room, she turned away, giving the door a lazy pull as she made for the lounge.

It closed behind her with a thump she hadn't intended, making her jump and turn. But the door hadn't swung fully shut; the noise she'd heard came not from behind but in front of her, and it wasn't the sound of a door but a footfall on bare wooden stairs. Someone was coming up to the flat.

She was almost in the lounge before the steps faded, but that was because they were being muffled by the landing carpet. Helpless, she stood clutching her bag at her chest in self-defence.

What now? She could hide, but where, and would it do much good anyway? It would only make matters worse than they already were. Unsure what to do, which way to turn, she did nothing. Numb from head to foot, unable to move, Maggie stood her ground while, across the lounge, the door knob turned and the figure moved into the room.

24

She didn't wait to see his face. The slow inward motion of the door was enough to spark her into action again. She found her legs just in time; turned back along the corridor, brushing past the slightly ajar bedroom door. Briefly, she thought about continuing to the kitchen, but there was nowhere to go from there. Instead, she ducked to her right, into the bathroom, easing the door shut as quietly as she could, pressing her full weight against it as she slid the bolt silently across.

At least a locked door now stood between her and whoever had entered the flat. She assumed it was Bryce; who else could it be? If she'd hesitated in the lounge one second longer, she would've known for sure, but that might've been a second too long for safety. She heard the main door closing, and soft slow footfalls somewhere inside the flat.

Now, she thought. Get a grip on yourself. You've bought yourself maybe a minute – two at the outside – before he realizes you're locked in his bathroom. If he's desperate, and God knows, what you've seen so far in this place means he is, he won't think twice about breaking this door in. So what do you do? *Reason* with him? Plea bargain? And then? Hell, if he's guilty – if he did anything more than spy on Julia, photograph her, phone her anonymously – then he'll say anything to put you at ease. He'll wait until you feel safe with him, and then you'll unlock the door, and he'll be standing there like the grim reaper himself, blade in hand, and you won't have a second chance, no way.

The footsteps moved closer, then seemed to fade inside the bedroom. It wouldn't be long before he noticed the change in there; one of the photographs was missing, a detail *he* wouldn't miss.

In desperation, Maggie cast a glance about the bathroom. The bath, to her left, was built into an alcove, obscured by a large sectioned shower screen. At a pinch she could hide behind the screen until the threat passed, but the bath would be the first place he'd look. That reduced her options to one. The window over the toilet was small, though not too small to keep her from scrambling through. The window ledge above the cistern looked high, but certainly reachable if she stood on the toilet seat. It was either that, climb out of the window and deal with whatever came next – a fifteen-foot descent to the street, either shinnying down a pipe or falling – or wait here like a good girl and face the consequences.

She was edging past the bath when she heard movements again – more than footfalls this time. She could hear someone breathing, hard and fast, as if suffering from asthma or panic. This is it, she thought. He's seen it; he's seen the gap on the wall where the photograph should have been, and now he's trooping through to the kitchen to check the notes in his file. She felt a presence flash past the bathroom. But the sounds that followed pushed her another step nearer to terror: first, the leaden steps across the kitchen's bare boards, then a clatter of cutlery as a drawer was swept open with force, and something – a knife; it could only be a knife – was removed.

He knows and he's coming, and God help you if you don't get your act together *now*. As the footsteps clumped back across the kitchen, not lingering near the table – presumably he didn't have to check the file to know that his pages were gone – she rushed towards the window.

That was when it happened. As she took a hurried step forward, her left heel hit a damp patch on the linoleum, skidding, skewing all her weight to the left.

Funny, she thought, and the thought must have passed through her head in an instant; funny, but *all* the floor's gleaming wet. Even as she fell, she was aware of how much water there was. In an hour or three, the puddles should have evaporated. The shower or bath must have been running quite recently, and had probably overflowed.

The shower screen checked her fall, and the edge of the bath kept her from tumbling the rest of the way. It dug squarely into her hip, sending a lance of pain clear up her left side to her shoulder. Maggie gasped as the screen pitched aside, clutched the bath's edge with her right hand, dipped her left for balance, and felt lukewarm water up to her elbow. When she recovered her footing, she saw what she'd very nearly fallen into.

The bath was full, and judging by its temperature hadn't been run more than an hour ago. The water was still clear as crystal, unclouded by soap, which was why she was able to recognize the corpse floating face-up so easily.

It was Carl Bryce, the train-spotter. Only it couldn't be him; it couldn't be because Bryce had just taken a knife or some other deadly weapon from the kitchen and was now poised outside the bathroom, so close to the door she could hear him catching his breath.

No, no, no, go away, she thought, blinking through a blindness that might have been fear or tears or both. You're just an illusion. This isn't happening. Please disappear.

Bryce shifted in the water, but only because she'd brushed against him while withdrawing her hand. He seemed to be winking at her, although he couldn't be seeing. He was wearing his train-spotter's dowdiest uniform: nondescript shirt, faded jeans, threadbare white socks and black loafers. Jesus, who on earth wore white socks with black shoes? It was in such lousy taste. His hair drifted on the surface like seaweed. His sightless eyes watched her without expression. There were pinkish smudges about his neck and throat where someone had held him. She waited for a sign of life, a faint movement of the lips, a bubble of air at one nostril, but there was nothing. At last she tore herself away, hand over mouth, wanting to retch, longing to let out the fear, the horror, unable even to breathe.

Help, please help me help for Godsakes help me –

The screaming was all in her head. Her mouth was open, she was gagging, but made no sound. All she could hear in this echo chamber was the faint lapping of bathwater, the occasional drip of the showerhead into it, and the breathing – not *her* breathing but the breathing on the other side of the door. The scream didn't force its way out of her until the door-knob turned, and by then she was on her feet and moving again.

She dropped her bag. Slithered on the linoleum as

she picked it up again. She didn't think what to do next. This was no time for thinking, only for doing – she'd done enough thinking to last her a lifetime. Thinking had led her into this mess; thinking had made a damn fool of her. She'd ignored Linda and Christine's advice only to follow her nose into blackness. She'd thought herself into a hole as dark and final as a grave.

And look at you now, look at you now, a small voice somewhere inside her head began mocking. You really believed you could *help* Julia, didn't you, but you can't even help yourself! You thought you could play detective, gathering clues like a farmworker picking peas, but –

'Shut up!' she cried, and the rattling of the doorknob became a sudden frenzy. It wasn't Carl Bryce trying to break in here, but someone unknown – someone far more terrifying. Carl was dead, undeniably, indisputably dead, and this person had held him beneath the water until he stopped breathing, no question. But why? And if –

You're thinking again, stop thinking, no time for thinking, no time –

In a flash she was standing on the toilet seat, leaning forward, wrestling open the latch restraining the window. The window dipped outwards and away from her as she pushed it, and cool damp air blustered into her face. She was beginning to feel trapped in a slow-motion dream. As she hoisted herself head first through the window, Maggie imagined she was leaving a tiny piece of her sanity behind, a little something to keep the train-spotter company. Good luck, Carl Bryce, wherever you are now. Good luck and goodbye.

The shock of the sight of the street below almost killed her, even before she'd started forcing her hips through the window space. She was more than half out before she sensed she might be going about this the wrong way. It was a long fall, and here she was, suspended in mid-air, no safety-net, the ground looming fifteen or twenty feet below. There was a ledge just below the window, and if she'd had the good sense to go out feet-first she could have lowered herself on to it. But, damn it all, when a madman attacks the door scarcely twelve feet behind you, you don't get to think these things *through*.

He *was* attacking the door now, and not with fists or feet. From where she'd managed to put herself, Maggie couldn't see past her midriff into the bathroom, but she knew the sound of splitting wood when she heard it. The killer was using some tool to prise the door calmly from its hinges.

Jesus, get *moving*. There was a drainpipe to her right, two, maybe three feet away. She could reach it if she could only angle her body correctly. When she twisted towards it, extending her right arm, her finger-tips brushed the edge of the pipe. Pivoting on her hips, she eased herself further through the gap an inch at a time. If she could grasp the pipe, and if the pipe was sturdy enough to take her weight, she'd be able to twist around until she faced the wall, release her legs and with luck get her feet safely on to the ledge. She'd found enough leverage to thread her fingers around the pipe when the bathroom door jarred and groaned behind her.

No, it wasn't through yet, but the first of the hinges had split free. She still had a few seconds. Each would feel like an hour, but she mustn't dwell on that, mustn't think, no more thinking from now on, God damn it! Now she was clutching the pipe while her full body weight pressed down on both shoulders. It felt like a ton, but somehow she managed to hoist herself upwards, half-turning to allow her right leg through the window. As her heel scraped through, she wobbled slightly, and her bag slid clear of her left shoulder, along her arm, and was gone.

Seconds seemed to pass before Maggie heard it hit the concrete below. Careful now. The next part was critical, because she had one leg inside and one outside, one hand free, one clinging so hard to the pipe her wrist was bursting. Slowly, gradually, she switched her grip on the drainpipe from right to left hand, allowing herself to turn fully towards the wall before lowering her free leg, toe scraping the brickwork, until she felt the ledge secure underneath her.

Fine, as far as it went. Now, at least, she was facing the right way, more or less, but she still had to hold on while she eased the rest of her out. A cramp seized her thigh as she tried to withdraw her left leg. At the same time she heard, inside the bathroom, the second hinge splitting from the woodwork with a dull, hollow thud. She prayed that the door had three hinges altogether; better still, four.

Maggie was back on two feet again, shuffling along the ledge until she could enclose the drainpipe with both hands. Her head was thumping; a rhythm as regular as any on V's crowded dance floor seemed to have made a home in her skull. But at least the difficult part was over. Now all she had to do was go down.

At first, she was unable to move at all. Cramp had turned everything between her waist and ankles into a series of tight, agonizing knots. When she glanced down, the ground rushed up at her, bringing prisms of swirling colour into her vision. Don't faint; for Godsakes don't faint! Later you can do whatever you like, but right now you've got to *move*, you've got to make yourself *move*.

The sound of the door giving way in the bathroom gave her all the incentive she needed. One quick deep breath, one whispered curse, and for a moment she was airborne; the soles of her shoes were off the ledge and then on the wall, either side of the drainpipe. She hadn't practised this manoeuvre before, and she'd never known how powerful gravity was, even at this height. It sucked her down six or eight feet, scouring her palms, before she was able to steady herself. After that, the rest was plain sailing. Shinning down another few feet, she jumped the rest. The ground flew up at her, and she landed, not too awkwardly, winding herself but – thank you, God – breaking no bones.

She was already running as she stooped to collect her bag from the ground; running, not looking back, not daring to. If she had she would have seen a face at the bathroom window, watching her go, and she didn't want to see that face – the face of someone unknown – as long as she lived. Though she still might, in her dreams tonight, if she ever lived long enough to dream again.

25

Maggie woke with a start, and at first she thought she'd been dreaming. Then the aches and pains insinuated themselves through her body again, and she knew. There *had* been a face staring after her as she ran from the house; she'd felt the steely gaze on her back as surely as she sometimes felt Julia's presence, and now she was angry with herself for not having dared to turn and stare back. If she'd plucked up the courage to do that one simple thing, she would now have a story to tell the police. She would have a full description to give. But instead she'd copped out.

And blanked out.

Some super-sleuth *you* are, the voice mocked her again. You can't even help yourself. Just look at you now.

She was lying half-dead on the couch in the lounge, and the half of her that was still alive felt too numb to function. How on earth she'd made it to the flat was a mystery, but here she was, half-swallowed by pillows, a blanket draped over her legs. She'd been crying in her sleep, and her eyes were still raw, her sinuses clogged. Thank God there was no one around to see her like this; thank God she was alone . . .

'At least you're not alone.' The voice came from

across the room, and a dim blur in the armchair nearest the window worked itself gradually into focus. 'I'm here if you need anything. Just rest for now,' Linda said.

'How did I . . .' She tried to sit up, and the knots up and down her legs tightened. 'Ouch. How did I get here?'

'Don't you know?'

'Not yet. Maybe it'll come to me.'

'Actually, I doubt it. I found you tripping over yourself on the street near the Uni. Could've gotten yourself run over, you damn fool. It's a good thing I was on lunch-break or you'd be lying in hospital now, not here.'

Maggie shook her head, bewildered, but even this slight movement caused her to wince.

'You were stumbling about like a drunk,' Linda was saying. 'Couldn't control your legs, and the cars were slowing and hitting their horns while you sleepwalked in front of them. In the end I had to bundle you into a taxi and bring you straight here. The minute you were inside the cab you blacked out, and I had to get the driver to help me upstairs with you. Cost me extra in waiting time for the privilege. What were you *doing* back there, Mags?'

'Trying to get away,' she said quietly.

'From what?'

'From *him*, from whoever –'

'Don't exert yourself any more. You're not making sense. We'll talk about this later, because right now –'

'It can't wait, Linda.' Maggie forced herself upright, ignoring the pain. 'You have to call the police. I was at

Carl Bryce's place and and . . . There was water on the floor and he was in the bath and –'

'Carl Bryce was in the bath?' Linda's eyes narrowed.

'Yes, but he was dead. He *was*. Someone – someone got there before me, and then, while I was still in the bathroom, they came back. And I had to – I had to –'

'Slow down. You're confusing me. What did you see?'

'He'd been strangled, I think. Or drowned. Or both. It was . . . Linda, you've got to tell the police.'

Linda was already on her feet, snatching up the phone. Dialling, she held the receiver to her chest, shooting Maggie a look of pure anger. 'You're an idiot, Mags. Didn't I ever tell you so? God knows, we invited trouble when we let you into this place, didn't we?' Then her gaze softened. 'I thought you and Christine were going there together. Couldn't you have waited, for crying out loud?'

'I only wanted to talk. I never expected –'

Linda nodded and told the receiver, 'Police, please.' After a moment she physically stiffened, turning her back on Maggie. Maggie closed her eyes, drifting into the grey while Linda began. 'Ahm, yes. I have to report a – well, I guess this is murder. A friend of mine found . . . Right; sorry. It's Linda Hollis. Hers is Maggie Waverly. She's here, but she's not really fit to come to the phone right now. The address? What? Ours or the victim's?'

Maggie listened while Linda fed the officer the barest of details, interjecting only when Linda needed clarification. Just before Linda hung up she said, 'Tell him this is all about Julia. Tell him to get Penhaligon to come. I should talk to him.'

'Right.' She relayed the message, and Maggie heard the phone thump down.

'I've got evidence,' she murmured, half asleep. 'I don't know what it means, but –'

'Sssh. It can wait. They'll be here soon.' Linda's voice was hushed and solemn.

'I want you to be here when they come. You and Christine.'

'Christine's got a late lecture. Heavy day for her today. I'll be here, though. Get some rest for the time being, why don't you?'

'I should be at work. They'll be wondering –'

'I called them already. Shut up.'

'And I'm missing a shoe,' Maggie slurred, drifting again, but this time Linda didn't reply.

She was vaguely aware of the shoe having slipped off her foot, but she couldn't visualize where. She'd probably lost it on the way upstairs; or in the cab, or on the street earlier. Julia had lost a shoe too, she remembered. Another coincidence, except there was no such thing as coincidence. Whatever else had ensued after she'd fled from the house had escaped her completely; she must have been close to blacking out even as she ran, purblind, towards the street, the traffic, Linda.

Thank God for Linda. Thank God for both her and Christine. She'd been living a nightmare, a nightmare which had reached its climax today, but she wouldn't have made it this far without them. Oddly, the last image in her mind as she slipped away wasn't that of the bathroom door splitting wide, or of Carl Bryce's body slumped in the tub: it was of the chaotic lounge where his desk stood scattered with paper, with the open filing cabinet beside it. The papers in those drawers were in one hell of a state. After all, what was the point of introducing a filing system only to leave it in chaos? Why had Bryce bothered?

There was an explanation, she knew. It should be obvious. But she was weak, the answer lay just beyond her, and now blackness moved over her thoughts like a heavy cloud blotting out daylight.

She must have been catnapping, because the sound of the phone hardly startled her at all. She thought she heard Linda's footsteps crossing the carpet to answer it, then a door whispering open somewhere while the ringing continued. Perhaps what she'd heard was the doorbell, for when her eyes flickered open the lounge was empty. No: wrong again, not the doorbell, because the telephone was purring in its usual reedy manner. It didn't sound like a bell at all. She was still half soaked in sleep, and her senses were playing tricks.

She slithered from underneath the blanket and stumped to the phone, kicking off her one shoe along the way.

'Hello?'

No reply.

Not again, she thought. Not *this* again. But here it was; familiar, cold, deadly as ever, a silent reply she thought she'd heard for the last time. Until this minute she'd assumed the train-spotter had made those calls, even if he'd stopped short of murder. He was the one who'd papered his walls with Julia, who'd been obsessed to the point of following her with a camera, but he was no longer in any condition to phone.

'Who the hell *is* this?' she bellowed.

'Maggie? D.I. Penhaligon. That's one novel way to answer, I must say.'

'I did answer. *You* didn't answer *me*.'

'Sorry about that. Gremlins on the line. We've installed this new switchboard system and I lost you for a second there. Everything all right?'

'Everything's hunky-dory! Couldn't be better! You got my message, I suppose.'

'What message?'

'You're kidding? What message? The one about Carl Bryce. Surely someone told you he –'

'You'd better explain this slowly, Maggie. To begin with, who is Carl Bryce? And what does this have to do with Julia Broderick?'

'It has a lot to do with her. In fact, I'd go so far as to say that whoever killed her did the same to *him* too.'

'Killed? Now, hold it right there, slow down a minute. You're way ahead of me. Start at the beginning again.'

She was about to explain when the connection stuttered, then fell dead altogether. Maggie stared at the receiver, aghast, until it finally struck her that Penhaligon might be trying to call back. She hung up and waited. A minute crawled by. She lifted the receiver and –

There was no tone at all. The line was dead.

The telephone company must have cut them off; but she'd written a cheque for her share of the bill only last week and Christine had paid the total on her way to the Uni. Perhaps she'd pulled the lead out of the phone socket. Taking the lead between her fingers, she traced it painstakingly around the room, behind a chair, along the base of a wall, under the carpet past the kitchen door. She'd almost reached the dim alcove beyond, when she sensed someone moving towards her, and stiffened. Then she heard the outer door close softly, and she was face to face with Linda.

'Jesus,' she said, gasping, hand on heart. 'You made me jump out of my skin.'

'I'm sorry, Mags.' Linda was smiling, but her eyes appeared heavy and troubled.

It took Maggie a second or two to realize that someone was standing behind her: Marcus. When he shifted forward into the light, his features seemed as coolly impassive as she remembered. She shuddered to think of the other night, her moment of weakness, his cold embrace.

'What on earth were you doing?' Linda asked. 'You're supposed to be resting, damn you.'

'There's a fault on the line. I was trying to trace the lead to the socket.'

'Let me.' Marcus coaxed the wire from her fingers. 'If you're as sick as Linda says, you ought to lie down. You don't seem capable of taking *anyone's* advice, Maggie. What makes you so obstinate?' He stood just inside the alcove, watching her.

Ignoring him, Maggie turned to Linda. 'I was talking to that policeman just now, Penhaligon. We got cut off.'

'What did you tell him?'

'More or less what I told you, but I don't think he made sense of what I was saying.'

'I see.'

'He hadn't heard of Carl Bryce. He knew nothing about the report you gave on the phone.'

'That's odd.'

Maggie sat leadenly on the sofa, the lounge gyrating very slowly about her. Her bag lay on the floor to her right, and she dragged it towards her, began rummaging through it. 'But you gave Penhaligon's name, didn't you?'

'What are you looking for?' Linda asked quietly.

'The evidence I told you about. I found this at Carl Bryce's place. He was obsessed with Julia. He had a . . . Wait a minute.' She may have blacked out after the fact, but she clearly remembered having stuffed the diary extract and the snapshot into one of her bag's compartments. The photo was here, but the pages were missing. 'Where the hell are they?' She looked at Linda, bewildered.

'You won't find them there.' When Marcus spoke, a feeling of cold dread stirred in her even before she knew what he meant. 'You have to understand, we couldn't allow you to show those pages to the police,' he said. 'We just couldn't.'

Then, dropping her gaze, Linda said, 'Mags. I'm so sorry it has to be this way. It isn't what I intended, believe me.'

26

As the truth slowly dawned on her – not that she wanted it to; she was trying with all her strength to shut it out – Maggie thought she heard thunder, except that the sound was inside her head. All at once she understood everything. She remembered how Linda had frozen that first night, the night Maggie came to view the flat, as if she'd answered the door to a ghost ... because, in a way, she *had*. And how withdrawn she'd seemed the night the film crew were doing their thing. It was now all too clear why she'd broken down afterwards, half-accusing Marcus, half-confessing, and why she'd refused to come to Carl Bryce's today. But, of course, Linda *had* to refuse: by the time Maggie arrived at the place, she'd been there already herself. And, of course, she hadn't called the police to report a killing. She'd called Marcus.

The very idea seemed too outlandish, too impossible. But it's true, she thought. It's true, because these are the people who killed Julia – and now they're going to kill her all over again, they're going to do to you what they did to her, to keep you from telling what you know. But what *do* you know? What do you *really* know? Oh, Jesus ...

The room swirled slowly about her, soft at the

edges. Marcus coughed dryly, cast the telephone cable aside, and seated himself on the arm of the couch next to Linda.

Linda closed her eyes and sat back, pinching the bridge of her nose between thumb and forefinger as though nursing a headache. 'It isn't what it seems,' she said finally. 'This wasn't some ugly, malicious scheme that we cooked up between us. It was nothing like that.' She reached for Maggie's hand, and Maggie recoiled. 'I'm sorry if I let you down. You're still my friend, and I still care about you. This doesn't make any difference to us.'

'Of *course* it does. How can you say that?'

'You shouldn't have pushed so hard,' Marcus said. 'Everything would've been fine if you'd kept your nose out of it.'

'That's nonsense and you know it.' Maggie was too numb to be furious, and her words sounded dopey and slow. 'She would've come back to haunt you, no matter what. Do you seriously think I made matters worse?'

'Yes, in a way,' Linda said. 'By forcing us to look at her again. It was never going to be easy to get over her, but you made it harder. All we wanted to do was forget.'

'But you *killed* her, for Chrissakes! How *could* you forget? You killed her and then you did the same to Carl Bryce.'

'Maggie, please. I never –' Linda began, before Marcus cut her off.

'We were trying to survive,' he said, looping an arm around Linda's shoulders. 'We were fighting to stay together. There were so many pressures pulling against us. Maybe you won't understand but –'

'I don't. Who would?' Maggie shot him a poisonous look. Any moment, she was certain, she'd be violently sick. 'Those pressures were all your own doing. You ...' She turned quickly to Linda. '*He* slept with Julia while you were in Oz, didn't he? Well, didn't he? He threw himself at her, and whose fault was that? Hers?'

'There are two sides to every story,' Linda said. 'She'd shown an interest in Marcus long before that. Just flirting, I thought at the time, although I now know it was more than that. The fact is, Julia invited trouble. She attracted it like a magnet.'

'You're covering for him. You've been covering for him all along. But, Linda, why?' This time it was Maggie who reached for Linda. 'Just look at him, will you? He's got liar, cheat, and good-for-nothing written all over him. You *know* what he is. What on *earth* are you doing defending him?'

'Watch your damn mouth.' There was rage in Marcus's eyes; a rage that perhaps Julia had glimpsed as she drew her last breath; a rage that had driven him to dispose of the train-spotter too. 'You haven't the faintest idea who I am. Linda knows. She understands. But you? – you're nothing. Your *opinion* counts for nothing.'

Maggie returned his icy glare until she felt the dizziness surge again. To Linda she said, 'Is that how you see it too? After the things we've shared, the things you've told me about him?'

'What things?' Marcus wanted to know.

'Be quiet.' Linda brushed him away.

'You're trying to turn her against me too,' he seethed at Maggie. 'As if we haven't already been through enough –'

'You heard what she said. Shut up.' She could feel herself drowning, the shock pushing her under, but she wasn't about to submit without fighting. If she hadn't felt so totally empty, so weak, she would've attacked him with her own bare hands.

A silence spun out. Then Linda said, 'I think we should take a walk.' Rising, she went to the window. 'The sky's so much clearer than it's been all day.'

'But it's dark,' Maggie said. 'I'd rather . . .' She stopped herself there. As long as she remained in the flat, she was helpless. Marcus knew how much she knew, and he'd have to silence her, as he'd silenced Carl Bryce. Outside, though, she might find an opportunity to run; she could call for help, if she could summon the strength to do so. Was Linda offering her that chance? And if so, why? From her posture – rigid and still as she stared from the window, her back to the others – it was impossible to tell what she was thinking.

'It's better if we stay here,' Marcus said. His nervous gaze flitted between the two girls. 'Keep things in the family, so to speak.'

'I need to get out,' Linda said, still unmoving. 'I'm suffocating here.'

'Then *get* out. I'll stay here with her.'

'But the police will be coming. She spoke to that detective before.' She turned to face him, arms folded stiffly across her chest, eyes dark and downcast. 'I'd like to explain everything fully to her while we still have time. I owe her that much at least. We can't just leave it like this, Marcus, can we?'

'Fine. Have things your own way. You always did.'

Linda didn't dignify the remark with a reply. To

Maggie she said, 'Think you can stand on two feet? Freshen yourself up first, if you like. But don't try escaping out the window again. Your luck might run out this time.'

She couldn't believe this was happening, really she couldn't. The dream which the rest of the day had felt like had nose-dived further, into a nightmare in which she found herself unable to act, to scream, to make herself heard. This is so damn *civilized*, she thought, splashing her face with water in the bathroom, checking her anxious reflection in the mirror. You should be fighting, screaming from the rooftops, thinking on your feet. There are people in this building. They'll hear. They'll help. She watched the water swirl as she pulled out the plug. A few strands of black hair – Christine's, the slob – clung to the sides of the basin.

But screaming from the rooftops is what they *expect* from you, she thought. Wake up, for Chrissakes! You've still got your wits, and that's *all* you've got; you're physically no match for Marcus, and here isn't the place to put up a fight. If you have anything left, anything at all, you'd better save it. And for now play along. Play the game.

Maggie lingered at her dresser, lipstick in hand, conscious of the muttered conversation in the next room. Perhaps they were discussing where to take her, or even – she tried to shut out the thought, but it slipped through regardless – how best to dispose of her. Though she couldn't hear what he was saying, Marcus's voice sounded loud and irritable. Maybe he preferred to finish things here; or maybe – far more likely – Linda had convinced him that the police were coming, and he was suddenly restless to move. Well, let him wait, let him sweat. Right now, Maggie knew, time was her only friend. The longer she stalled, the better her chances.

She pursed her lips, stared into the mirror until her other self slipped out of focus. Half Maggie Waverly, half Julia. She added a touch of eyeliner to complete the illusion, and half-imagined Julia whispering, 'Hey, I'm *back*! Did you miss me? Did you really think you were alone, sis?' With a final flourish, Maggie picked up the lipstick again and scrawled in large letters across the mirror:

> *Christine, Police, Anyone –*
> *Help me now. Linda and Marcus are the ones*
> *who killed Julia. They know that I know and any*
> *time now I'll be –*

The door thundered open behind her, and she dropped the lipstick like a hot coal. Marcus, framed in the mirror, stood at the threshold. His dead eyes locked with hers in the reflection, and helpless, numb fear swarmed over her. Then he saw what she'd written, or started to write, and he was at the dresser, fingers clamping her wrists before she could move.

'Get off me, Marcus! Get your hands *off* me!'

He flung her aside as if she were nothing more than a limp rag doll, and she tumbled against the edge of the bed, twisting her right knee as she slid to the floor. When she raised her head again, the mirror was just a blurry red smear where Marcus had wiped his hand. Her words were gone for ever. And so, she reflected, when he'd finally calmed down enough to speak, were her chances.

'You shouldn't have done that,' he said.

27

Outside a light frost crackled underfoot as they walked – Marcus at her right hand, Linda at her left – from the house. A curtain shifted at a window across the street, but it was only an elderly resident shutting himself in for the night; even if he was spying, he didn't care.

You could scream now, she thought, and no cavalry would come. People might hear, but wouldn't ask questions. All right, fine, you can't scream but can you run? Do you have the legs to carry you? And once you start running, do you know where to go? Helpless, flagging, she was in no fit state to resist.

'Don't try anything,' Marcus whispered, reading her mind, hot air escaping his lips like smog. His right hand twitched, buried deep in his pocket, and if it wasn't a knife he was holding there, then it must be some other tool of death; a hammer, a length of cord stripped from the phone line. She'd already crossed him. Once more could be fatal.

'It was me,' Linda announced as they reached the street corner, turning right towards the busy Hunslet road. 'If you want to lay the blame in someone's lap, start here. No one's exactly innocent in this story, Mags, but some of us are more guilty than others.'

'I don't want to know this,' Maggie said, but Linda was miles away, her voice a cold, vacant monotone.

'Julia was my *friend*,' she was saying. 'You have to believe that, or nothing else I tell you will make sense. She was my friend, so I knew she was anything but perfect. I *tried* to forgive her over Marcus, I *tried* not to let it ruin everything. I told her, Yes, I understand your feelings about Hayden and that this is just some stupid blip, that you threw yourself at Marcus on the rebound; I realize how hard it is to make something work when you're so far apart; but you're going about this the *wrong way*. You're toying with Marcus, and he's too dumb to see it.'

Marcus gave a low, disapproving grunt. 'Thanks a lot.'

'And Julia?' Maggie said.

'She agreed that's what she'd been doing. It was nearly over between her and Hayden, and she'd turned to Marcus for some kind of reassurance, isn't that so?'

He nodded. 'But I was missing you too. I needed someone, and you weren't there.'

'She was using him,' Linda went on. 'At least to begin with. I don't think she ever really understood she was punishing me, hurting me. When I flew back from Oz it was obvious that something had changed. You could feel it in the air, and Chris was so withdrawn and so distant, as if she wanted to tell me but couldn't. It took weeks before Marcus caved in and admitted everything.'

'"We'll kill her if this goes on any longer,"' Marcus murmured obscurely, staring straight ahead. 'Those were Julia's exact words. She knew from the start we were wrong to get involved. We both did.'

'But you still let it happen,' Maggie said. 'Why?'

This time it was Marcus who sounded far away, his thoughts drifting ahead of him. 'She had a kind of power over people, Julia did. She wanted love and admiration and she always got what she wanted. It was a knack she had, the way some people have a knack for sports or figures or art, you know? She had a knack for making people fall for her, and I was one idiot who did.' After a beat he added, 'But they broke the mould the day they made her.'

'I know,' Maggie agreed. 'I know.'

Linda said, 'What nearly *did* kill me was when I found out that it wasn't really over after all. People can be such liars sometimes, Mags, I swear. But I'd never imagined friends could be that way. It was a miracle Marcus and I were still together – being cheated destroys your trust, you *expect* things to go wrong, you don't believe anything anyone tells you. All this hot air Julia came out with about going to Cambridge, to Hayden – that was the *last* thing on her mind when she moved out. It was a lie.'

'Then she and Hayden *were* finished after all. She wasn't leaving to get married.'

'She lost control,' Marcus said. 'Didn't know what she wanted any more. I saw her one night at the Uni after she and Hayden split – they'd had this difficult, long-distance separation – and she told me she needed space, needed time to recover. But it was more than that: she still wanted to be with me. At first I didn't know how to take the news – we'd already agreed it was over between us – but I guess she just needed someone to hold on to . . . She'd got it into her head that being away from the others, from Linda and Chris, would make it much easier to see me.'

Maggie felt herself sinking further into the grey. This wasn't the Julia she'd come to know; less the gutsy, confident, self-possessed role-model she'd heard Christine – even Linda – raving about, more like the Julia Dave Sessions had spoken of. Close to the edge, was how he'd described her. Virtually insane. And as the bridge approached, some distance ahead, her thoughts returned to Sally in Rico's, and her parting words:

Ask your friends, why don't you? Ask them what she was really like.

You've had this all wrong from the start, she thought. And now you're paying the price for being so gullible. If Marcus is telling the truth – and why shouldn't he be? What can he lose by lying now? – then Julia *wasn't* the angel you've taken her for; she wore another face under the mask. Charismatic? – yes. Beautiful? – no question. So many things you've always dreamed of being. But insecure, deceitful – so many dark, negative qualities too. Jesus, to think . . . to think you wanted to *be* her!

Well, at least you'll be closer to being *like* her in a minute: you'll be united with her in a watery grave, because the bridge –

The bridge was patched with darkness. A couple of goths paced ten or fifteen yards ahead, but Maggie hadn't the strength to call for help: in any case they'd probably think she was crazy, or fooling. About half-way across she sensed Linda slowing to look at the star-spangled water. It was to happen right here, then. It was now or never, her chance to run might not come again. Then Marcus closed his fingers over her arm, and the urge to flee passed, her body became lifeless and weak again. The dust had settled, the die was cast. Whatever happened now, however terrible, had always been meant to be. She accepted her fate.

'Sometimes I see her in the water at night,' Linda murmured, half to herself. 'She's thrashing and kicking, with the water all around her, trying to swallow her whole, and I want to reach in and pull her out, but I can't. I'm too late. There's no bringing her back, no changing what happened. There's no changing anything.' She'd slowed to a standstill, and when she turned towards Maggie her silhouetted head looked crested with stars. In a low, straining voice she added, 'It's time to tell you what happened.'

'Linda . . . Please . . . Don't say any more.'

'You need to know. It's because you were so determined to find out that we're in this mess, am I right? You're forcing it on us. We didn't *want* to have to relive it.' She was weeping now, and in the darkness her eyes and cheeks shone dully. 'The night she came to the flat – that last night, the one we've had to go through again and again – was the final straw. The phone call she made? It was Marcus she spoke to, at Richie's. And you know what her last words were to me before she left? I'm sorry, she said. That's all. She just opened the kitchen door and whispered, so that Chris wouldn't hear, I'm sorry, Linda.'

Anger, not terror, raised Maggie's voice to a shout as she turned on Marcus. 'How could you? You *saw* her again, after all you'd put Linda through? God damn you!'

He sounded defensive, flustered. 'I had no choice, because on the phone she said that if I didn't go she'd do something we'd all regret later. She was out of control. She spoke in a kind of normal, even voice, but underneath I could tell she was close to hysteria. I'd already said I couldn't see her again, that I didn't want to lose Linda, but . . . she would've thrown herself off this bridge if I hadn't agreed, she really would. After the call, I just had to get out. I borrowed Richie's old VW and took a long drive to blow the cobwebs away and think everything over.'

Maggie's gaze fell on the black river. For a moment she half-imagined herself jumping, doing what Julia had only promised to, but Marcus's grip on her arm remained firm, and now he was steering her further along the bridge.

Cars breezed past, through the back streets, like spectres. Rap music thundered from one open window, speed metal from another, the outlined heads of their passengers nodding in time. The confusion of sounds faded as they turned left on to Sovereign Street.

Linda said, 'I tried calling Marcus, but he'd already gone. So I finished preparing supper, couldn't face eating, then headed over to Richie's to wait. I couldn't tell you more than this before, don't you see? I couldn't explain what was going on. I tried to imagine a best-case scenario, but everything looked so hopeless and black to me, and after a few drinks and card games I couldn't wait any more. When it turned midnight and Marcus still wasn't home, I ran – I mean, literally *ran* – to Julia's place. And that was how . . .' She trailed off, one hand swiping gleaming tears from her nose. 'The first thing was, I saw Marcus waiting outside the bedsit where she was staying. So I stood watching from the shadows across the road where he wouldn't see me, and while I really wanted to go to him I couldn't . . . I had to see what was happening. He was standing there, stamping his feet and rubbing his hands to warm them. Maybe ten minutes later, this white car turned up and Julia scrambled out. She was shouting and squabbling with the driver, and she slammed the door and the driver sped off, tyres screeching. Then she caught sight of Marcus and went to him – actually hobbled because she had only one shoe on – and put her arms around him, and . . .

'I closed my eyes at that point. I didn't want to see anything. My mind was racing. I felt like death. I didn't know what to believe any more. I shut my eyes and covered my face with both hands, and when I looked again Julia was opening the front door and the two of them were heading inside.'

'I'd agreed to meet her there,' Marcus said, 'because I didn't want to be responsible if anything *did* happen, if she did do something foolish. What I wanted was to reason with Julia, but she – she'd been drinking and a lot of what she was saying didn't make sense. She was accusing me, blaming me for Hayden or something. When I tried to tell her we could still be friends, but I wouldn't let anyone come between me and Linda again, she started to boil. She threw a few things, and I remember a vase missing my head by inches, and the sound of the thing smashing and then the doorbell ringing. So much madness.'

Linda gave a slow nod. 'She was ready to fight by the time I got inside. In fact she didn't want to let me in at all – Marcus did – and she was trying to blockade the door, and screaming, "This is none of your business, get out!" Everything just escalated, became more and more surreal, and the next thing – I don't know how this came about ... we were standing in her room, a small cramped space with a shower unit in one corner and a sink right beside it and the bed up against the opposite wall. And Julia ...' She was forcing herself to continue in spite of the tears, in spite of the horror she must be seeing again. 'Julia was smashing her things, throwing down glasses and plates and CDs, and I said to her, Please don't, we love you! But she laughed – a bitter, scornful laugh I still can't get out of my head – and looked me square in the eye and said, Screw you, you'll never get him back, not now; you're nothing to Marcus, and I'm taking him from you. How do you like *that*?

'I couldn't think. I really couldn't function for a minute. Somehow I believed – or feared – what she told me. The only thing in my mind right then was rage, and I lashed out at Julia, and ... Jesus, this is hard ... never connected, I swear. She flung herself aside, but slipped somehow and whacked her head against the sink as she fell. And then, and then –'

'It was as if the world stopped,' Marcus said gravely. They were on Neville Street now, where the traffic was denser, and he was raising his voice to make himself heard. 'She didn't move at all, didn't make even a sound. There was a tap dripping into the sink, which was all I could hear. And then Linda sank to her knees and said, Oh my God, oh my God, see what we've done.

'It wasn't her fault, but right then, right there, it didn't feel like an accident. It felt ... premeditated, and we panicked. I sent Linda home and took care of everything else myself.'

'And how,' Linda said quickly. 'She had one shoe

missing, and Marcus dressed her in those stupid pumps she'd borrowed from Christine. He forgot to get her into her coat. He hadn't a clue. Later, he took her away in Richie's car. In case anyone had seen either of us arrive at the house, it seemed better if she was found elsewhere. As it turned out, someone saw him *leaving* with Julia. The whole thing was botched from start to finish.'

Maggie shook her head, appalled. 'Jesus, if you'd only left her where she fell, people would've *assumed* accidental death.'

'Would they?' Linda flashed her a quick glance. 'Hindsight is twenty-twenty, right? If only we'd done things this way or that. Instead, we managed to make an accident look like murder. Don't think we didn't replay it differently in our heads later on, but at the time . . . Wait, we can go now.'

Checking quickly left and right, she darted into the street as the traffic further down Neville Street slowed for the lights. Maggie had to struggle for balance as Marcus dragged her along behind, his fingers clamping her arm firmly enough to make her squeal. Then, as they reached the far side of the street, she caught sight of a sign for Granary Wharf on the stone wall under the railway bridge, and at once understood where they were leading her. But of course: where else but to a place where her screams would be muffled by overhead trains, by the busy street near by, by the pounding of water under the arches?

'Linda, please,' she said, but Linda was already trooping ahead, through the gaping walled entrance, out of earshot.

'It's very quiet at night here,' Marcus was saying. 'I

like to come sometimes in the summer after the traders have gone. It makes me feel peaceful.'

Well, fine, but Granary Wharf felt anything but peaceful to Maggie just now. A numbing, blustery wind whipped between the black walls, the thunder of water some distance ahead transforming the place into the location of someone's nightmare. Her own.

This wasn't how she remembered it. Seven days a week, scores of traders and shoppers turned the Wharf and its alternative clothing, art and bric-à-brac stores into a kind of Bohemian paradise. It was a place she'd always regarded with fondness, but not now, certainly not now, because now she was being bundled against her will through a tunnel, black as a bad dream, the kind of tunnel people on operating tables supposedly passed through in their minds when they left their bodies. Even the tiny amber spotlights, fitted high on the walls beneath the rising curve of each arch, seemed to be fading into themselves in the dark. Ahead, where she knew the shops and galleries were, Maggie could see only deeper shadows. She could hear only water rumbling under the icy stone floor.

'Linda, why?' she protested.

'Why what?'

'Why me? Why does it have to be like this?'

Linda shrugged. It was a good thing, a painfully good thing her face was obscured by the darkness. She still sounded tearful. 'Do you think you've left us any choice?'

'You *do* have a choice. Yes, you do. The same choice you've had from the start. Please listen. This can't go on. The killing can't go on. What happened to Julia *was* an accident.' Her voice was pitched almost to breaking-point. 'But Carl Bryce's death never was. You murdered him.'

'He brought it on himself,' Marcus said. 'Julia became an obsession for him, and she did for you too. She was bad news, don't you see? Anyone who ever tangled with her suffered one way or another. Haven't you realized that yet?'

She was trembling, sobbing, unable to contain herself. 'But why kill Carl Bryce?'

'We had to,' Marcus said, 'because he saw everything. He followed Julia everywhere. He took candid pictures of her; you've seen them, of course. He even kept a diary. They'd met in the Student Union canteen. She must've smiled or small-talked for a while with him, and although she forgot him like that –' His fingers snapped in front of her face. '– he took it to heart, read her friendliness as some kind of come-on. This was a year ago, easily, and for a year Carl Bryce pursued her, pestered her, phoned her. You're mine, he kept telling her. You're mine. And he must've believed it. The bastard just wouldn't leave her alone.' Marcus drew a leaden deep breath. 'In fact, those words, *You're mine*, kept echoing through my head all the time I was getting her ready for the car. I put them right here, like so . . .' Maggie flinched as his fingertip scrawled circles on her brow in the dark. 'I figured it was something we could use against *him*, if we had to.

'The night this all came to a head, he was at her again. He'd caught her outside V as she was going in, and she told him to get out of her face before she called the police. It didn't make any difference. He followed her home anyway. He was there when Julia took me inside; he was there when Linda left, half an hour later. It's all in his diary. I took most of the pages from his filing cabinet. You found the rest.'

'He'd taken photos of us too,' Linda explained. 'He told me as much in a phone call he made to the flat. I doubt whether any came out – it was pretty damn dark and we would've noticed a flash, so he couldn't have used one – but when you're under that kind of pressure it's hard to see logic.'

Maggie swallowed, her mouth sour and dry. 'What did he say?'

'That he had photos, and other bits and pieces that he could use against us if he wanted to, but that he was going to sit on them for a while, let us sweat. What? I screamed at him – really screamed down the phone. You're blackmailing me, you sick little sleaze? He said no. He wanted nothing from us, but we'd taken Julia away from him and he intended to make sure we paid for it, in his time, in his way. The world is full of twisted souls, Mags, believe me; I know at least half of them. When – when you said you were planning to see him, I *knew* he'd spill everything he knew; and if he didn't at first, you'd soon drag it out of him.

'I panicked. Ditched my first lecture and called Marcus.'

'And Marcus . . .' Maggie's head was swimming. The thunder of water and wind filled her ears. Dizzy, almost drunk with fear, she could barely prise the words from her tongue. 'And Marcus broke into the flat and tore it apart looking for those papers and snapshots. Then he killed Carl Bryce in cold blood.'

'Not necessarily in that order,' Marcus said, his voice so cool and aloof and final she could only dread his next move. 'No, I killed the little cockroach first. Then I searched the flat.'

'And now me.'

'And now you.'

'Linda?' she pleaded, one last time, but Linda had fallen silent. She had turned her back.

'So,' Marcus said, 'you know the whole story too. Well, the story ends here.' At last he released her arm, and the fingers of his right hand prodded her firmly beneath her breasts, winding her. She took two deft steps backwards only to realize, too late, she was now on the brink of the gushing water.

She was standing flush against the rail overhanging the torrent. It was black and loud, swollen by days of rain, and the spray prickling her skin told her how agonizingly close she'd come to being truly like Julia. At least Julia was already dead when Marcus lowered her into the river; at least her death had been quick, so quick she'd had no time to fear or consider it. Jesus, Maggie thought, even now you're envious of her, of all the breaks she had that you never had! Please let this be over soon!

'Will this ever end?' she wondered, and that was when she sensed, in the gloom, Marcus lunging towards her, seconds before the screaming began. It wasn't until his hands found her throat that she realized the screams weren't her own.

28

What happened next was so much chaos. Days would pass before she'd be clear about the order of things, the sequence of events which followed. The hands at her throat were cold and hard as metal, and she couldn't hear Marcus's breathing, though his face was just inches from hers. It was drowned out by everything else.

A confusion of noise filled her head. Even the traffic beyond the dark arches seemed lost to the pounding of water and the voice – not her voice, it couldn't be hers, for she was choking, gagging for air – rising to a shrill, fragile scream which multiplied to a chorus under the arches.

'Enough!'

That was what she heard, she was sure; but Marcus didn't seem to agree. His hold on her was unrelenting, so powerful she felt herself being pushed down and backwards, straining the rail behind her. Her spine would fracture if this lasted much longer. In her mind, she saw lights rush towards her like stars. Enough, she thought. Enough is enough. Even Julia hadn't bowed out this way; but Carl Bryce certainly had, and these were the hands that held him under the bathwater, sent him to unhappy oblivion.

'Marcus, for Chrissakes!'

The voice made more sense to her now. She thought she recognized it, though it seemed so far away, but *she* was far away too, drifting towards the light at the end of the tunnel through which she was starting to pass. The voice was Linda's. It couldn't be Christine's. No one knew they were here. Had she come to her senses? If so, too late, Maggie thought. She was already taking leave of her own.

Perhaps drowning felt something like this. They said that to drown was a fine way to go, not at all as dreadful as it seemed from outside. Once you were past the pain threshold – an excruciating pain as the water rushed in and your lungs filled – a dizzy, gentle sense of relief took over. You started to float. She was floating now, though she hadn't yet hit the water. In her mind she was soaring far away, further away and, briefly, she hovered somewhere above herself, surrounded by orange lights, and saw, through the dark, Marcus pressing his full weight against her, forcing her backwards over the rail, her back arching impossibly, her hands clawing feebly at his, then falling lifeless and limp at her sides. And another figure, behind Marcus, tearing at his shoulders to drag him clear.

'Enough!' she was screaming, Linda was screaming. 'We can't . . . You can't . . .'

Linda had finally reached her limit. She hadn't killed anyone, though she'd suffered as if she had, and she simply couldn't endure any more. Marcus was just getting started, however; he'd developed a taste for murder, and that was the darkness Maggie had seen in his eyes from the start, a darkness she'd found so attractive the night he kissed her and she now saw clearly for what it was: a cold and murderous spirit.

She felt no pain now. She hadn't the slightest urge to resist. Her body was violently rocking, but that was because Linda was struggling with Marcus, whose hands were still fastened at Maggie's throat. She felt a spiralling dizziness as if she were falling. She felt herself snap back into her body. Then came the switch – an impact she felt in her bones as if someone had dropped a huge weight on the ground just feet away.

'You bastard,' Linda was sobbing. 'Enough, I said, and you wouldn't listen, you wouldn't listen!'

Slowly, Maggie returned to herself. The vice at her throat had slackened, and suddenly Marcus's weight was lifeless and sluggish. The next thing she knew, he was beside her, pressing forward against the rail; then behind her, below her as the waters engulfed him.

The spray covered her face like a cooling breeze. Somewhere off to her left she heard Linda murmuring strange, senseless words to herself. She sounded ragged and hoarse, and there was something in her hands, some dark solid object that glinted, amber-coloured, as she lifted it, then vanished as she cast it into the waters below.

'What . . .' Maggie could barely croak out the words. She could still feel the pressure of Marcus's grip. 'What did you do?'

She flinched as Linda moved nearer, then collapsed lightly against her. She spoke in whispers between sobs. 'He's all right. He'll be all right. I didn't . . . didn't kill him, but I had to stop him. Took the hammer out of his pocket. It was meant for you, if he needed it. And I –'

Her cries sounded like the start of some long, upward-spiralling scream. Instinctively, she buried her face against Maggie's shoulder until Maggie felt the heat and the moisture of tears against her own skin.

'He just wouldn't listen,' Linda murmured. 'I had to, I had to . . .' It was almost the voice of a lost child, timid and wavering, and Maggie understood there was nothing more to fear. She touched Linda's hair and held her. Finally, when Linda lifted her head, her words were easier to decipher. 'He'll get out at the bank further down. All I did was stop him, but not for long. He'll be back, Mags. You ought to get moving. *Can* you move?'

She could, she thought, though she doubted she'd be able to sprint for a while. 'Why did you do that?' she wanted to know. 'What made you change your mind?'

'I wanted to stick by him, really I did. But Carl Bryce – I never planned for that. I thought Marcus was going up there to find the diary and photographs. I never believed he'd do what he did. Knowing made it nearly impossible for me to go on. And now this – now this. I really didn't want to see it through, but I nearly did, I really believed I would. You've got to believe me.'

'I do. I do.'

'God knows, there's a darkness in all of us,' Linda went on. 'Maybe sometimes it just takes over. Something changed in Marcus after he hooked up with Julia, that much I *do* know. It was something I never saw in him before, something *she* put there. Jesus, I loved him, but now . . . now I don't know where to turn. I've lost Julia. And now Marcus. And everything.'

'Not me.' Maggie winced as her throat contracted tightly. 'Or Christine. We'll stand by you.'

'Why should you care? After today? After everything?'

'I must be simple. Ask me another.'

They began, very gradually, to peel themselves away from the rail, supporting one another unsteadily back through the tunnel, under the black wind-filled arches to the light and the traffic ahead. They stood for a time at the entrance to the wharf, not speaking, watching an endless stream of cars and trucks flowing past in a blur.

'What now?' Maggie asked, searching Linda's face for a clue. 'Where does this leave us?'

'Everything seems so clear to me now,' Linda said. 'I'm so sick and tired of covering up. It's about time we set the record straight. Let's go home, Mags.'

The walk to the flat took less than fifteen minutes, though the same route to the wharf had felt like a journey of days. As soon as the house came into view, Maggie noticed the light at the window, which could only mean Christine was home. They were still some distance away when Linda stiffened, taking hold of Maggie's arm.

'See there,' she said. 'They're waiting.'

So they were. Two vehicles – a police patrol car, D.I. Penhaligon's BMW – were parked in front of the flat. Just like the movies, Maggie reflected. The police always arrived too late.

'Where do we go from here?' she asked.

Linda shook her head and looked down. 'Let's go in. I'm not planning to run. There's nowhere to run *to* any more. It's over.' Briefly, she threw her arms around Maggie, holding on as if for dear life. 'I'm going to miss you, sis. Really I am.'

'Me too. It won't be the same without you.'

'It's time,' Linda said, letting go, smoothing imaginary creases from her jeans. Then they strode to the house, towards change, towards whatever the future held in store.

29

Maggie forced herself to watch from the doorstep while Linda was driven away.

Seated in the rear of Penhaligon's BMW, she didn't protest and didn't glance back at the house as the vehicle accelerated along the street. She stared straight ahead as if too exhausted to care any more.

It's not over, Maggie thought with a shudder. For her, it's only just beginning and there's no end in sight. Does this nightmare *ever* end?

By the time the BMW vanished from sight, the street had become a watery blur in her vision. Tearful but still alive, she followed Christine upstairs to the aroma of fresh coffee and muted grunge music. Christine switched the CD for something quieter, more appropriate.

For a time they sipped from steaming cups and gazed into space. Less than two hours later the telephone rang. Marcus had been dragged from the water, alive but numbed by exposure. Right now, numb was a fair description of how Maggie felt too. It would take time – more than days – for this feeling to pass, if it ever did.

Three days later, when *Crimewatch* was broadcast, the Julia Broderick reconstruction had been pulled from the schedule. Of course, it was old news by then, though local reporters still camped out in the street, or bombarded the flat with telephone calls until Christine ripped the plug from its wall socket once again.

'I'm not going to let them get to you,' she said. She was standing in Maggie's room, Friday morning, while Maggie slumped at the dresser, aghast at her own pale, sunken eyes. 'Those vultures haven't the sensitivity to see you've been through more than enough already. I'm going to stay right here and protect you.'

'You should be in lectures,' Maggie complained. 'I should be at work. The world's going to hell while we're holing ourselves up here.'

'For now. But things will settle. We'll get over this, won't we, together? And life will go on.'

'It won't be the same. Not without Linda.'

'No, it couldn't be,' Christine said sadly. 'But it *has* to be different, don't you see? We're not supposed to replay the past. It just isn't meant to be. You should've learned at least that much from Julia.'

Yes, Maggie *had* learned. She'd grown in some way she couldn't yet grasp. If she'd gained anything at all from the whole awful experience, it was that she'd become her own person; she no longer needed to depend on Julia. When she stared at her reflection, it was Maggie now who returned the look, not Julia. More than ever, she needed to believe what she'd tried so hard to deny for so long. Julia had never been a suitable role-model. She'd always been less than perfect. She'd belonged to a world Maggie could never be part of, a world of desire and darkness; but her mystery would live on, like her story. She's not finished haunting you yet, Maggie thought bleakly. But she was sleeping again, and Julia seemed to have stopped whispering to her, at least for the time being.

One morning, a week or so later, she took the black dress that she'd worn to V and elsewhere to a charity shop on the Headrow and mailed the leather shoulder-bag to Julia's parents, enclosing a note, which read simply:

> *Dear Mr and Mrs Broderick*
> *I never knew your daughter but I often wish I had.*
> *She was much loved by everyone who did cross her*
> *path. I followed her story closely, and though there's*
> *nothing any of us can do to change things, I do wish*
> *you all the very best for the future. Here's to better*
> *times. I enclose Julia's bag, which she left behind*
> *when she vacated the flat at the above address.*
> *Since it was a personal item of hers, I thought you*
> *might like to have it.*
> *Yours,*
> *Maggie Waverly*

Her name, thank God, had been kept from the papers. Once the police had charged Marcus with Carl Bryce's murder, local journalists seemed to lose all interest in her. In a matter of days the phone calls ended too, the vultures disappeared from the street.

She resisted running back to her parents. Over the course of three short phone calls to home, she'd managed to keep the truth to herself. Everything's fine, she'd assured them. Did you hear the news and wasn't it terrible? She'd tell them everything soon, of course, as soon as she could, and when she did they would hit the roof. Her mother would beg her to return to the nest. But she'd deserted the nest once and for all and this was the real world now. In the real world you had to learn to be strong to survive, and she *had* survived.

And soon she'd be stronger still. Work would take over eventually. She'd transfer her belongings to Linda's room, and some new tenant would move into Julia's. The vacancy had already been advertised. It was going to be fine, really it was. She was leaving it all behind. Almost all of it.

Ian called. Ian pleaded to see her again. Eventually she gave way, remembering her promise, and suddenly there she was facing him across the table at Stefano's wine bar again. It wasn't until then – until she found herself meeting his stare and not being fazed or weakened by it – that she realized how far she'd travelled.

'That's quite a story,' he agreed when she'd finished telling it. 'Thank God you're all right, Mags. You could've been . . . Anything could've happened to you.' After a pause, his eyes downcast, he added, 'You really need someone to look after you, Maggie.'

'No, I don't. And that's the whole point. I don't *need* anyone, Ian, not any more.'

'After all you've been through?'

'Especially after all I've been through.'

'Will I see you again?' He was clutching at straws now. 'Is there any chance, when you're over all this, it'll be just like it was before for us?'

'Do I have to spell it out?' She was trying to be forgiving, but his sorry manner, his defeated tone, made this almost impossible. 'If *you* weren't so dependent on me, or anyone else for that matter, it might've been easier. But no, Ian. You'll suffocate me, I know you will. I'm sorry. I'm sorry it didn't work out with Alison but –'

'She just wasn't what she seemed at the time,' he said quietly.

'Is anyone?'

He gazed at her blankly. Even now he failed to understand. 'So what happens next? Is that it? We just say our good-byes and call it quits?'

She managed a smile; even reached for his hand. 'We've changed,' she said. 'Or maybe it's just that I have and you haven't. I don't know. But you'll meet someone else, I know you will. You never had too much trouble that way.'

'It won't be the same.'

'It shouldn't be.' She took a deep breath. 'I hope things work out for you, Ian, really I do.'

Then she left him. He didn't follow or try to leave with her, and when she reached the stairs leading out of the basement she forced herself not to look back. She didn't want to remember the look in his eyes as he watched her go.

The first thing that struck her when she noticed the white Ford Fiesta in the pedestrian precinct outside was how unshocked, how unmoved she was by the sight of it. The engine was running – a small cloud of carbon monoxide chugged from the exhaust – and the driver, Dave Sessions, leaned out the window, half-smiling, immaculately dressed as ever in a beige suit, powder-blue shirt and print tie.

'It *is* you,' he said. 'I thought so.'

'Of course. Who else?' She moved to the car, leaning in at the window. 'What're you doing here?'

'Trying to bypass the traffic. Failing miserably, of course,' he added, nodding at the shoppers blocking his route to the main road. 'It's Maggie, right? I'd recognize you anywhere, even without the make-up.'

Self-consciously she smoothed her cheek with the back of one hand. You're your own person now, she reminded herself. Your very own person. Confident and in control. No need to feel vulnerable because you're not her.

'If you don't mind me saying, this is quite an improvement,' he said. 'Making yourself up to be like Julia didn't really become you.'

'I realize that now. I just didn't then. I'm *not* her.'

He fell silent for a moment. 'So is everything all right? I heard they caught up with the ones who . . . you know.' He sighed and gazed sightlessly down the precinct. 'Still, we don't know the full story yet. I expect sooner or later it'll all come out in the wash.'

'I'm sure it will.'

'It's just good to know it's over at last, and to see that you're safe. Now you and your friends can look forward again. It must have come as a great relief.'

'I still have mixed feelings,' Maggie said truthfully. 'Right now I don't know *what* to feel.'

Dave Sessions gave a curt nod as if he understood, and checked over his shoulder as a pale-blue transit eased past, gradually parting the sea of pedestrians. 'Well. Good to see you. Really good to see you.'

'You too.'

He cleared his throat. 'Can I offer you a lift? I'm on my way home from work, but I'm in no hurry.'

'Some other time, perhaps.' She answered without a flutter of doubt. Maybe she'd never see him again, but how would it seem if she said yes? It would be like falling at the first hurdle; giving up all that she'd gained. She now had the power to do what she wanted, be what she wanted.

'Sure. Some other time, then,' Dave Sessions replied. 'You have all the time in the world.'

Dead right, she thought. Time to heal, to live and learn, and sooner or later even these memories will fade, become manageable. But never completely. Nothing so devastating could ever fade completely. If only Linda had been so fortunate. If only Julia had. God bless you both, she thought. You'll always be with me. Always.

Maggie Waverly took a deep breath and one step back and watched while Dave Sessions edged the Fiesta into gear, let out the clutch and drove from the precinct.